The Shadows of Rookhaven

Other books by Pádraig Kenny,
published by Macmillan Children's Books

The Monsters of Rookhaven

ACMILLAN CHILDREN'S BOOKS

The
Shadows of
Rookhaven

PÁDRAIG KENNY

ILLUSTRATED BY EDWARD BETTISON

Published 2021 by Macmillan Children's Books
an imprint of Pan Macmillan
The Smithson, 6 Briset Street, London EC1M 5NR
EU representative: Macmillan Publishers Ireland Ltd, 1st Floor,
The Liffey Trust Centre, 117–126 Sheriff Street Upper
Dublin 1, D01 YC43
Associated companies throughout the world
www.panmacmillan.com

ISBN 978-1-5290-3171-3

Text copyright © Pádraig Kenny 2021
Illustrations copyright © Edward Bettison 2021

1 3 5 7 9 8 6 4 2

A CIP catalogue record for this book is available from the British Library.

Printed and bound by CPI Group (UK) Ltd, Croydon CR0 4YY

This one is for Mona, who taught me everything I know about whispering in the corner at parties. We miss you, Momo.

MIRABELLE

UNCLE ENOCH

AUNT ELIZA

ODD

GIDEON

AUNT MAVIS

DOTTY & DAISY

PIGLET

Part 1
Billy and the Worms

Billy

'We loves you, Billy Catchpole. Your mum and dad loves you – you know that, don't you?'

Billy sat cross-legged in the gloomiest corner of the cellar. *Mum*, as she liked to be called, was sitting in one of the old, mouldering armchairs he'd rescued from a bombed-out house. Its once-bright floral pattern was faded to a pale yellow and grey.

'We loves him, don't wc, Dad?' she said, turning her eyes to the man sitting in the matching chair across from her. The man's head was tilted upwards. He was clearly distracted, as if not completely present in the room. Billy could see the sharp edge of his Adam's apple in his scrawny neck. It bobbed up and down as he tried to form words.

'That's right, Mum,' the man said in a hoarse whisper, his white, sightless eyes staring up at the ceiling. 'We loves him very much. And we loves his little sister too.'

Billy looked over to the corner where Meg was playing with a filthy rag doll. She looked no more than six years old, but appearances were deceptive for their kind. She had likely looked that age for a very long time – certainly from before he'd found her, anyway. Her hair stuck up in dry, jagged clumps and her soft, round face was grimy with dirt, but her eyes shone, and it made Billy's heart melt to see them.

Mum licked her lips, and the corner of her mouth twitched into a grimace as she tried to form a smile. Billy knew exactly what was coming next, and the thought of it made his stomach flip.

'You know what I'd like, Dad?' Mum said.

'No, what's that?' Dad replied.

Billy's shoulders and neck tightened, as if tensing for a blow.

'Something nice to eat. A snack, maybe.'

Dad frowned, then his face started to twitch and become more animated. He swung his head round on his stalk-like neck and looked towards Mum.

'A snack,' he whimpered, his hands clenching the armrests of his chair.

'Just . . . just something small,' said Mum, licking her lips again. She started to drum her bony fingers against the arms of her chair.

'That'd be nice,' said Dad, turning hopefully, desperately, in the direction of Billy.

Billy stood up, his eyes going to the book he was holding. It had been nice reading it. It was a book about pirates and treasure on a mysterious island, and it made him feel as if he were there on that island, and not here in the damp and gloom of the cellar with the Catchpoles. The book was written by someone called Robert Louis Stevenson. It was wrapped in a ragged and torn red dust-jacket. There was a pirate on the cover. He held a bloodstained sword and was looking at a smoking ship on the horizon.

'What would you like?' Billy sighed, barely able to look at them.

'Something small,' wheedled Mum.

'A snack,' said Dad.

'Just a little one.'

'But warm.'

'And juicy.'

'And *alive*.'

Dad rubbed a hand across his chin in an effort to wipe away a long string of drool that had been slowly dripping down from the corner of his mouth.

Mum leaned her head in Billy's direction. Her whole spindly body was quivering.

'What about a nice suckling pig?' she said, clapping her hands together with glee.

Dad responded with some vigorous nodding.

'I'll try,' said Billy, feeling the great weight of their expectation.

Mum smiled, revealing a mouthful of yellow, sharpened teeth.

Dad looked suddenly crestfallen. 'But not a dog. I hates dogs. Awful stringy things. Sour-tasting, they are. I hates them,' he shouted, banging a hand down hard on the arm of his chair.

'No dogs,' said Billy.

Dad's eyes widened. 'You promises?'

'I promises,' said Billy.

Mum clasped her hands under her chin and squealed,

her feet tapping the floor with delight. Meg looked up sharply from her doll and frowned at her.

'We'll stay in and watch the telly while you go about your business,' Mum said.

Billy looked at the old television set, which he'd positioned at a point between them. Its screen was caved in, and its casing was scarred and burnt. It too had been salvaged from the ruins of another house in the London streets above.

'Telly, yes. We'll watch us some telly before tea,' Dad murmured, his tongue licking his long incisors, his gaze returning to the ceiling.

Both of them settled back in their chairs, their breath rasping in the gloom as they returned to a state of what looked like semi-hibernation. Billy watched them for a moment. Secretly, he called them the Worms. Years of hiding underground from the sunlight that was fatal to their kind had bleached them both to a deathly pallor. They reminded him of white twisting maggot-like things, blind and panicked, oblivious to the world around them, caring about nothing else but their next meal. Nevertheless, he felt some measure of pity for them. It was hard not to after knowing no other company for so long.

They didn't speak of their past, but sometimes Billy would catch Dad rambling deliriously in his sleep about being banished by their family for the sin of hunting humans. About having broken something called the Covenant. They'd taken the name Catchpole years ago.

Slowly but surely, they'd started to imitate the ways of the people who lived in the world above. The telly had been one way of doing this, the furniture another. Soon he was calling them Mum and Dad. It was easier that way. Easier to pretend that how they lived was normal. He could have left them a long time ago, but he had no one else. He was alone. Even in his first couple of years with the Catchpoles he'd still felt alone, but at least he could imagine he was part of something bigger. A pretend family wasn't a real family, but pretending was better than nothing.

Meg was the only person in Billy's dark little world he truly had something in common with. He'd found her hiding in a rubbish tip. One look at her was enough to tell him that she wasn't human. She, too, had obviously been abandoned. No doubt for the same reasons he had. He'd offered her food, but she clearly had no interest in it, and being in sunlight didn't seem to affect her either, just as it didn't affect him, unlike the Catchpoles. He'd taken her home that very night and their 'family' had been complete.

Billy went over to Meg and knelt before her. He cupped her face in his hands.

'You behave now, Meggie. Stay here and look after Mum and Dad. Billy's going to see if he can get some food for them. I'll read to you when I get back.'

Meg rubbed her nose vigorously with her hand. Billy smiled at her.

He made his way up the stairs. Every step away from the Catchpoles seemed to make him feel lighter, and yet every step away from Meg almost caused him pain. They were all he had, and the world above wasn't safe for him. It wasn't safe for any of them, which is why they'd spent so many years underground.

The Catchpoles had found him years before, in the abandoned ruin of a house destroyed during the Blitz. Like him, they were discovering it was harder to find places to hide, what with all the people seeking shelter from the bombs. Almost anything below ground that could be converted to a shelter had been, which had left their kind scrabbling above in the dark and, in the worst cases, exposed to sunlight.

Some of their kind. Because he really wasn't exactly one of them, was he? He was what Mum called 'something else', just as Meg was. He was different. He could walk around in daylight for one thing, and pass himself off as human.

At least to the untrained eye.

He opened the cellar door just a crack and peered into the scorched shell of the house that sat above them.

Nothing moved, but Billy knew you couldn't be too careful. He hoisted himself up and over the lip of the opening, and then gently closed the door behind him. He made his way to the back of the house and crept out into the ragged garden.

It was dusk, and the light in the evening sky was a pallid pinkish grey. Billy sniffed the air. It was cold and a little smoky. To his right he heard the human family three doors down chattering among themselves.

Billy made a run for the bin at the end of the garden. He leapt on to the lid, and bounced straight up and over the wall, landing deftly on his feet in the narrow weed-tangled laneway on the other side. He crouched there for a moment, sniffing the air again and listening hard. He could hear the chatter again. A child laughing, a man speaking, someone saying something about it being teatime.

Billy moved swiftly down the laneway to the right, keeping his eyes and ears open. He was walking past the house he'd heard the noise coming from when he felt that familiar tug at his heart. He stopped, and looked at the wooden door that led into their back garden. He heard a child squealing with glee.

Just a minute, he thought. *I'll take just a minute to see. Just a quick look.*

Billy put his eye to the knothole in the door. He could see the well-tended garden and in through the window of the sitting room.

The father was standing by an armchair and smiling. He'd obviously just come in from work. He was still wearing his work clothes, a grease-splattered set of brown overalls. The young boy ran into the room like a little blond whirlwind, and his father ruffled his hair. He was followed by an older girl. She looked to be about seven, and seemed a lot quieter than her brother. Their mum was already sitting on the couch, and the children went to sit either side of her.

Billy knew every rhythm of this tradition.

The man leaned down towards the rectangular wooden cabinet with the grey screen inset in its front. This was the fabled family television set. Billy smiled as he remembered the excited shrieks of the two children as their father had lugged it in through their hallway a mere two months ago. It was made of scuffed and battered mahogany and the family seemed to love it.

There was the familiar clunk as a black knob was turned, and a tiny square of light appeared and then expanded to fill the full screen. The screen glowed with a low luminosity, and Billy saw the grey-black figures of two men onstage talking to each other. There was the laughter of what sounded like dozens of people, and the family, all of them sitting together on the couch, laughed along too.

Billy watched for a few moments, noticing their bright, shining eyes, their easy smiles and laughter. His own smile faded as he remembered the cellar and his 'family' below and what he had to do. He reluctantly stepped away from the door. He heard the laughter fading behind him as he walked, and felt that familiar sick longing in the pit of his stomach.

He rounded a corner that brought him to the front of the street. A few of the houses were empty shells, but some of them, like the one he'd just been spying on, had people living in them. Billy could see the warm glow of lamps through net curtains, and the telltale flicker of television screens.

He walked with his head down, making sure to avoid

any passers-by. The street was almost deserted, but he still didn't want to catch the eye of anyone. He passed by the Regal cinema. A young man dressed in the buttoned blue tunic, bow tie and pillbox hat of a cinema usher was sweeping the marble steps. He had a cigarette clamped in his mouth and he frowned as he spotted Billy. Billy averted his eyes and quickened his pace.

Billy had been in the Regal several times before, but had never once paid the admission fee. He remembered a Saturday night not long ago when he'd sneaked in and the place had been so packed it had felt fit to burst. A film about a hapless store assistant had been showing. The man in the film wore his cap backwards and was always getting into scrapes and falling over. The laughter was deafening. Tears were streaming down people's faces. There was a young couple sitting next to him and they were doubled over with laughter. Billy sat back and smiled at the screen, and just for a few moments he pretended the three of them were there together, and that they were a family.

A cold gust of wind rounded the corner and slapped a scrap of newspaper against his shin. Billy brushed it off and kept walking, leaving the Regal behind.

He stopped short as he heard whimpering on the air. Billy closed his eyes and listened hard. There was the rapid, panicked thrumming of a heart nearby. Billy nodded to himself and followed the sounds. The wind shifted slightly and he caught a scent. He quickened his pace.

The sound was coming from a dank alleyway nearby.

Billy crept into it, and something flashed in the gloom. He spotted a pair of eyes.

A dog's eyes.

I hates dogs.

Billy sighed.

It was a skinny-looking terrier, and it was pulling at a bone lying underneath a pile of mulch and soggy paper.

'All right, boy?' said Billy.

The dog's head whipped round. It looked terrified. Billy bent down and held his hand out. 'All right?' he said.

The dog eyed him warily, but started to approach him. It looked at him suspiciously for a second, then licked the palm of his hand. Billy smiled.

'Good boy.'

He could hear Mrs Catchpole's voice now.

Break its neck, Billy. Snap it like a twig. It won't feel nothing. It'll do as a snack. I ain't picky.

Billy's smile disappeared. He felt a shiver of disgust. He stood up.

'Go on, boy, go. There's a good boy. Run.'

Billy made to step aside, but the dog was trembling now, and it bared its teeth as it started to growl. It was staring at the mouth of the alleyway.

Billy cursed himself for not having paid attention. He should have noticed the alleyway getting darker. Should have smelled the scents.

A net descended on him, and one of the two men who now rushed into the alleyway tried to cinch it tight.

Billy could see him grinning. He stopped grinning when Billy punched him. The man fell backwards, choking and clutching his throat. The dog snapped at the man for good measure before it dashed away. Billy had just wrestled the net off himself when the other man swung at him with something heavy and black. Billy ducked, and in the same swift movement reached up and grabbed the man's hand. For an instant their eyes locked.

Billy squeezed.

Hard.

There was the splinter and crack of finger bones.

The man's eyes widened and he shrieked in agony. His weapon clattered to the ground. He fell back against the alley wall and slid down it, clutching his mangled hand to his chest.

Billy ran.

He could still hear the choking sounds and the other man howling behind him. He allowed himself a brief smile.

He stopped smiling as soon as he saw two more men burst from cover behind a parked van, and hurtle across the street towards him.

He pivoted on his heel, reached out and grabbed a drainpipe. He swung himself up and scampered skyward, feeling a curious mixture of dread and elation. He reached the eaves of the roof of a tenement building and flipped himself up and on to it, as if he weighed nothing. He heard someone shout, 'Get it! Get the feral!' and he was already leaping the space between the building and another one across the alleyway. He felt the rush of wind in his hair.

Something snagged his ankles, and now he found himself tumbling over and over, while the ground rushed up to meet him.

He tried to right himself in order to cushion his fall, but his ankles were tied together with rope, and he could see the wooden balls of a bolas wrapped round his legs.

The ground was wet and hard, and he hit it with a smack. For a moment, the edges of the world burned a vivid white. He couldn't breathe.

At last, he took in a huge lungful of air. It felt as if a knife had been plunged into his chest.

Then the rage came.

He felt the blood fizz in his veins. His breathing became guttural and the fingers of his hands became elongated and clawed.

Billy sat up and snarled. He worked at the bolas rope, took it off and swung it at one of his attackers, just as the man was about to pounce on him. A ball hit the thug in the side of the head with a loud *thok* and he flailed backwards into the deserted road.

The other man grabbed Billy's arms and tried to pin them behind his back. Billy snapped his head back and heard a satisfying crunch as the man's nose broke. The man groaned and fell on to the path with a slap.

Billy leapt to his feet.

'Stay still now, boy.'

Billy turned. A tall man wearing an ankle-length leather

coat was approaching. He had long, lank black hair, and his eyes glittered with a mixture of faint amusement and contempt. His hands were covered in tattoos.

The hair on Billy's neck prickled. He could feel his teeth elongating, the bones of his jaw almost cracking as they broadened. The muscles on his arms pulsed and hardened. His snarls became deeper and more animalistic. He clenched his fists, jutting his chin out, daring the man to approach him.

The man shook his head. 'Look at you. There you are now,' he said in a tone that sounded like something close to admiration. 'You ever felt hungry?'

The question stopped Billy in his tracks. The man smirked.

'No, don't suppose you have. No interest in meat, bone or gristle for you. Not for your kind, anyway.'

Billy was confused. How did the man know what he was? Billy tensed, and the man took half a step back.

'I wouldn't if I were you, boy.'

Billy leapt through the air.

The man held his palm up to his mouth and blew a fine spray of yellow dust in Billy's direction. The dust caught Billy in the face mid-flight. He felt as if he'd been whacked by a sledgehammer, and for the second time that day he hit the ground. He tried to raise himself up, but this time his arms and legs wouldn't respond. They felt dead and leaden.

The last thing he saw was the man looking down at him as darkness descended.

Billy woke with a start.

His head had been lolling on his shoulder, and he snapped to attention to take in his surroundings.

He was sitting on a chair in what looked like a large dilapidated warehouse. It had whitewashed walls and narrow windows boarded up with mouldering planks of wood. There was an enormous brass machine in front of him: a thing of shining cogs and gears and levers, with what looked like a large porthole of thick yellow glass at its centre. A panel of glass tubes in rows ran along the front. There was a lever in the centre of this panel. The long-haired man stood a few feet to the right of the machine, looking at Billy.

'It's awake,' he said.

Two men in lab coats were inspecting the machine's dials. One was a fresh-faced young man. The other was older, with dark hair going to grey. He wore half-moon glasses, and his eyes were a sharp, callous blue.

'Is that right, Mr Thorne?' said the older man, scribbling something on the clipboard he was holding.

'That's right, Mr Aspinall.'

Aspinall looked sharply at Thorne.

'*Professor* Aspinall.'

Thorne gave a dismissive sniff and sneered at the professor.

Billy tried to stand, but a sudden wave of nausea overcame him, and the world blurred to a sickly grey before his eyes. He collapsed back on the chair, gasping for air. His vision started to clear, and that was when he noticed the two golden clasps covered in runes clamped to his forearms.

'Wouldn't try moving so long as you're wearing them,' said Thorne, pointing to the clasps. 'That's some of my best work there. You won't be able to get too far too quickly so long as you've got them on.'

Billy went to grab one of the clasps to try to rip it off, but as he soon as he closed his fingers around its edge he was hit by another bout of nausea.

Thorne laughed. 'Wouldn't try taking them off, either. Unless you want to risk feeling like your head's come clean off.'

A door to the left opened and two more men stepped inside, flanking a middle-aged man in a dark coat and grey suit, who was walking with the aid of a mahogany cane.

The man with the cane had a boyish look about him. His cheeks were almost cherubic,

his nose slightly upturned. One of the men grabbed a chair for him and the man sat down on it, a few feet in front of Billy. He rested his palms on his cane and smiled at him.

'How very nice it is to meet you, Billy,' he said, his voice soft and gentle.

'Say hello to Mr Courtney, boy,' said Thorne, kicking the leg of Billy's chair.

Courtney raised a hand and looked pleadingly at Thorne. 'Please, Mr Thorne, that won't be necessary.'

Thorne stepped back, glowering.

Courtney was still smiling. 'Let me introduce myself, Billy. I am Robert Courtney. You may have heard of me.' Courtney raised an eyebrow. Billy shook his head. Courtney nodded and looked amused. 'Well, perhaps not.' He prodded a knot in the wooden floor with the end of his cane. 'My father was renowned industrialist Joshua Courtney. He passed his company on to me. And now with my family fortune I'm helping to rebuild London after the horrors of the war.'

Billy clenched his jaw. He wanted to be out of this place, but there was something about this man that seemed to demand his attention.

'I myself suffered during the war.' He tapped his leg. 'A shrapnel wound, hence the cane.' He nodded to himself and smiled ruefully. 'But here I am.' He gestured at Billy. 'And here you are.'

Billy was aware that all eyes in the room were on him. Professor Aspinall was tapping a pencil on his clipboard.

'Why have you brought me here?' asked Billy.

Courtney leaned forward. 'Because you're special, Billy. You have certain talents and skills. And because I need your help.'

Billy clenched his jaw and narrowed his eyes. 'Why should I help you?' he hissed.

Courtney cocked his head at the two men who'd come through the door with him. 'Gentlemen, if you would be so kind.'

The two men walked back out through the door.

Courtney smiled apologetically at Billy. 'Billy Catchpole. How whimsical and charming that all of you should see fit to give yourselves a family name.'

Billy felt a cold sensation that flared to a hot, sweaty panic when he saw the Catchpoles being ushered into the room by Courtney's two men. Both of them had their wrists bound with rope. Courtney's men urged them forward with cattle prods, and the Catchpoles' eyes rolled agitatedly as they tried to get their bearings.

'Where is we, Mum? Where is we?' Dad wailed.

Mum gave a sudden sob. 'Billy's here. Our Billy's here!'

Dad sniffed the air. 'Oh, praise be. That he is. That he is.' Dad changed direction and started to shuffle towards Billy. 'Maybe he's gone and brung us a nice suckling pi—'

The force of the cattle prod into his back threw him off his feet. He yowled in agony on the ground, twisting and turning like an eel. Billy was surprised when he almost leapt from his chair. He was even more surprised by the tears that pricked the corners of his eyes.

Dad was dragged to his feet, and he and Mum were pushed towards the machine. Thorne had opened a hatch in the side of it by means of a valve wheel. The Catchpoles were ushered in, clutching each other fearfully, looking around in a blind panic, mouths working silently behind the glass. Thorne tightened the wheel behind them, and there was a clunk as the door locked.

'What are you doing to them?' Billy asked, panic rising.

Courtney nodded to Professor Aspinall, who pressed some buttons then pulled the lever. The machine hummed into life, and Billy felt the floor beneath his feet vibrate. Courtney was looking almost hungrily at the scene as it unfolded. A light sheen of sweat had formed on his forehead, and Billy could hear the man's heart starting to pound faster and faster.

The humming of the machine rose to a loud, pulsing *vworp vworp* sound that reverberated through Billy's skull. The air around the Catchpoles started to shimmer with purple and mauve light. They held each other. Billy could taste lead on his tongue.

The *vworp*ing sound came in waves now, and the light around the Catchpoles became more vivid. Billy saw them blinking sightlessly.

And then he watched, horrified, as they crumbled to fine, swirling dust right before his eyes.

Courtney clenched and unclenched his hand on the pommel of his cane, his eyes still on the viewing window.

'Incredible,' he almost sobbed. 'Incredible.'

Billy felt a terrible hollowness in his gut as he took in the scene. He slumped forward.

Aspinall pushed the lever up. Pressed the buttons. The sound stopped; the colours faded. There was silence in the room except for the soft hissing of a luminous green vapour that now seeped into one of the glass tubes inset into the machine's control panel.

Professor Aspinall twisted the tube and detached it from the machine. He brought it over to Courtney, who took it in trembling hands, gazing upon it with a mixture of terror and hope.

'I wouldn't be too confident, Mr Courtney. The subjects were rather weak and old. The degradation in active essence will be quite acute.'

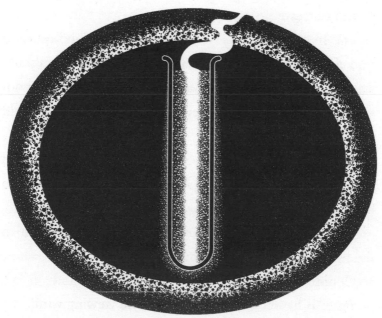

Courtney didn't seem to hear him. He smiled for a moment, but that smile started to fade as the green vapour within the glass tube began to blacken.

Aspinall nodded. 'I told you, sir. Very often degradation can—'

Courtney screamed and hurled the tube on to the floor where it shattered into a thousand pieces, black vapour seeping into the air. Courtney's hair flopped down in front of his eyes, and he brushed it back in agitation.

Billy was panting now, looking at the black vapour as it disappeared into nothingness. *All that remained of Mum and Dad, gone.*

Courtney smiled at Billy again, but it was the tight trembling smile of a man on the edge.

'Like I said, I need your help, Billy.'

Billy's nostrils flared as he tried to contain his anger and grief. *Was that grief?* He thought so, and it surprised him. Even though they weren't strictly 'family', Billy felt something for the odious Catchpoles. How could he not after all these years in their company?

'I'm not helping you with anything,' he said hoarsely.

'Oh, but you are, Billy. You very much are,' said Courtney. 'I have so much money I don't know what to do with it. I can have anything I want. You, on the other hand, grew up with nothing. No home. Not even a proper family. I can give you a home, a home of your own. Somewhere you'll both be safe.'

Both? Billy felt another wave of panic at that word.

'Otherwise *she'll* go in the machine,' said Aspinall.

Courtney rapped his cane on the floor. One of the men who'd escorted the Catchpoles left the room and returned seconds later, guiding Meg in with a hand on her shoulder. Billy felt as if he'd had a bucket of ice water thrown over him. He tried to stand, but another wave of nausea gripped him, and it felt as if the inside of his head were filled with jagged glass splinters. He tried to call on his feral nature, but he felt weak, as if that part of him had been suffocated by the magic of his bonds. Meg went to run to him, but the man with her wrapped his arm round her. She started to cry. The nausea passed and now Billy roared at the ceiling until he was hoarse. He finally gave in and slumped in his chair, panting, tears streaming down his face.

'Let her go,' he croaked.

Courtney shook his head. 'Not until I get you to promise me something, Billy. Otherwise she goes in the machine.'

'I think that would be a rather interesting experiment,' said Aspinall, eyes hard and ruthless as he looked at Billy.

Billy lowered his head and looked at the floor, tears of frustration blurring his vision.

'What do you want me to do?' he sobbed.

Courtney smiled sympathetically. 'It's very simple. I just want you to use your talent for stealth and cunning to steal something for me.' He turned towards Thorne. 'Mr Thorne, if you would be so kind as to release our guest.'

Thorne came towards Billy and pressed down roughly on each clasp with both hands until there was a clicking sound. As soon as he removed the cuffs, Billy's head felt clearer. Meg was still sobbing. Billy looked at her. Their eyes locked and he nodded. She understood his unspoken message for her to hush. She bit her lip.

'Do you have the device, Mr Thorne?' asked Courtney.

Thorne reached into his coat and took out a silver-plated orb, no bigger than a fist. He handed it to Courtney, who held it in front of Billy.

'This will aid you in your task,' he said.

Billy said nothing.

Aspinall sniffed. 'It's this or the machine, boy. You choose. Choose right and you and the other urchin get your freedom and a life to live as you please. But if you double cross us, Mr Thorne here will find you, and then it's the machine for both of you. I can't say I wouldn't be curious as to what it would do to you. You are, after all, both part beast and part human.' Aspinall smiled. 'It would be quite an interesting experiment, I should think.' Courtney glared at him. 'Professor, please.' Aspinall pursed his lips and gave a little deferential nod, but Billy could see the anger in his eyes.

Billy stood up slowly. It was an effort to look at his captors. His head felt like lead on his shoulders.

Courtney stood up too, and held the orb out towards him. It was covered in strange runes, similar to the ones on the clasps. Billy took it in his hand. It felt heavier and more dense than an object of its size had any right to be.

Courtney placed a hand on his shoulder.

'I want you to use this to find something very precious.'

'Where do you want me to go?' asked Billy.

Courtney smiled at him.

'I want you to go to a place called Rookhaven.'

Part 2
The Misbegotten

Mirabelle

Mirabelle watched the horse-drawn carriage emerge from the portal. It made its way up the Path of Flowers and through the main gate. Moonlight glinted off its polished black surfaces as it rocked from side to side.

'Couldn't she just have left the horse and carriage behind like everyone else?' asked Mirabelle.

Enoch looked down at her. 'Aunt Mavis always likes to make an entrance. "Elegance above all else" is her motto.'

Mirabelle shook her head. There was an eddy of air and a whiff of something metallic as another smaller portal whirled into existence between them both. Odd popped out of it, looking flustered. He was panting slightly.

'Well, that was a delight,' he said.

'You took a while,' said Mirabelle.

'She spent some time considering which carriage to arrive in,' said Odd.

'And you pointed out to her that there was no need for one?' said Mirabelle.

Odd nodded. 'Frequently. In the meantime, I have also been attempting to source more items for the Great Configuration.' He looked pointedly at Enoch. 'After all, I have been kindly volunteered to fetch, carry and escort family members from their various homes.'

'But you do it so well,' said Enoch, without taking his eyes off the carriage.

Odd sighed. 'I miss the days when everyone arrived on foot. If I have to open portals for everyone in another hundred years it will be too soon.'

Guests had been arriving at the house in a steady stream all week. With each new arrival, Mirabelle felt her excitement mounting. The Great Configuration happened once every one hundred years and only in the Room of Lights. Enoch had told her that families from every sanctuary attended. He was old enough to have seen many of them in his long lifetime, but when Mirabelle asked him to explain exactly what the Great Configuration was he got a strange, faraway look in his eyes and seemed to be at a loss for words. Everyone she spoke to about it seemed to react in the same way.

'It's somewhat *celestial* in nature,' Eliza had said, but she wouldn't be drawn on the details, and she seemed to be close to happy tears just talking about it. The rest of Mirabelle's family appeared to have made a pact with each other not to ruin the surprise for her or Gideon. It was Gideon's first Configuration also. Her family's subterfuge only served to make her more excited to see what was to come.

'Aunt Mavis isn't that bad, despite what people might say,' said Enoch, muttering the last part of his sentence under his breath.

'She is,' Odd mouthed to Mirabelle.

'And there's Vernon and Byron to look forward to as well,' said Enoch.

'Yes, they're both delightful,' said Odd drily.

The carriage drew up in front of the house, and they made their way down the steps to greet its passengers. The driver was a short, hooded figure in a dark-grey cloak. He turned slowly to look at Mirabelle, and she caught sight of two glints of silver within the depths of his cowl. He seemed to regard her for a moment, then turned back and looked out over the horse's head as it whinnied softly, its breath pluming in the cold air.

Enoch held the door of the carriage open, and the first thing that greeted them was a high pitched 'Uoooeee!' from within.

A large white face loomed out from the interior.

'Aunt Mavis,' said Enoch. 'How lovely it is to see you again after so long.'

Mavis Dibble heaved herself up eagerly from her seat. Her sons sat either side of her, supporting her arms as she raised her massive bulk into a standing position. She had a wide mouth filled with razor sharp teeth, and a swirl of faded blonde hair piled on top of a conical head. Like her sons she had long slanted nostrils and no eyes, but this didn't mean the Dibbles were blind. Odd had explained to Mirabelle that they could see very clearly indeed. 'Another reason to be wary around them,' he'd added ruefully.

'Enoch, oh, Enoch, it has felt like forever. How long has it been?' Mavis cooed.

'Over seventy-five years, I think,' said Enoch.

'Seventy-seven. I've been counting,' said Odd. 'You favoured us with a surprise visit.'

Mavis gave a squeal so high-pitched that Mirabelle thought her eardrums might explode.

'Odd! Oh, darling Odd,' Mavis shrieked. 'Thank you so much for the use of your portal.' She flapped her hands with excitement while she waited for the driver to unfold the steps for her. 'Thank you, Winthropp,' she said to the hooded figure, taking his clawed hand as she stepped gingerly down the steps with a delicacy that belied her bulk, then tiptoed over to Odd. She pinched his cheeks and thanked him again, while wondering aloud if she might be permitted to use his portal for 'the occasional trip abroad'.

Odd, to his credit, bore the attention as stoically as he could, while the Dibble twins looked on, grinning all the while. They were very tall and both wore pin-striped suits; one a deep blue, the other a murky brown and orange. Both of them wore spats that coordinated with their suits. Their long, delicate fingers moved languidly, like the tentacles of sea anemones, as they watched their mother shower affection on Odd.

'You'll fetch me something nice soon, won't you?' said Mavis, giving one of Odd's cheeks a particularly hard squeeze.

'Of course, Aunt Mavis, anything for you,' said Odd, giving her a smile that didn't reach his eyes.

Mavis clapped her hands together. 'Oooh, isn't he a

darling?' She turned towards Mirabelle, nostrils flaring again as she sniffed the air.

'And who might this be?'

'This is Mirabelle,' said Enoch.

Another shriek from Mavis. 'Ooh, Mirabelle! The famous Mirabelle. How lovely to make your acquaintance.'

Mavis stepped towards Mirabelle, pushing the twins aside to get to her first. She bent towards her with her hands clasped together in what looked like a gesture of prayer and thanks. 'Mirabelle,' she said in an awed whisper as both twins lined up behind her.

The edges of Mavis's nostrils flared and flapped with a movement that Mirabelle found slightly perturbing. She clasped Mirabelle's hands in hers. 'We are so very pleased to finally meet you.'

'Very pleased,' said the twin in blue, leaning over his mother's right shoulder.

'And intrigued,' said the one on the left.

'Oh yes, very *intrigued*,' said Mavis.

Mirabelle felt strangely discombobulated. It was a very disconcerting thing to have someone without eyes 'look' at her, but nonetheless she felt Mavis's sharp gaze drilling into her, and it made her skin crawl.

Mavis let go of Mirabelle's hand and wiped her own hands with a pink lace handkerchief. Mirabelle thought this a strange thing to do.

'This is Vernon,' said Mavis, nodding to her right. 'And this is Byron.'

'We've heard so much about you,' said Byron.

'So much,' echoed Vernon.

'What you did, ridding us of that . . . that . . .' Mavis stopped, her mouth wrinkling in disgust.

'Monstrosity,' finished Vernon.

'Obscenity,' agreed Byron.

Mirabelle felt her cheeks getting hot as the trio loomed over her. While still 'looking' at Mirabelle, Mavis handed her handkerchief to Vernon between thumb and forefinger. He deposited it gingerly into the inner pocket of his jacket.

Mavis made a flapping motion with her fingers. 'And where are your friends?'

As if on cue, Lucius descended smoothly from the sky and landed on Mirabelle's right shoulder. He looked back and forth between the Dibbles with his good eye, then seemed to dismiss them as he rubbed under a wing with his beak. Mirabelle suddenly felt a lot more confident.

'This is Lucius,' she said.

'He helped you, didn't he?' said Mavis.

'He did,' said Mirabelle, feeling suddenly very possessive of the raven, and reluctant to reveal any more information.

'And how long ago was that?'

'It's been five years, Aunt,' said Odd.

'Imagine. Five years. How could I have forgotten? Why, we've counted every day, haven't we, boys?'

'Every one,' said Vernon.

'Each day a gift,' said Byron.

'A blessing,' said Vernon.

'A veritable benediction,' said Byron.

Lucius cawed, but studiously avoided looking at the Dibbles. They were still staring at Mirabelle, and now there was a long, awkward pause, as if no one present knew what to say any more.

Vernon and Byron smiled politely and nodded. Mavis's mouth twitched for a moment, as if she were having trouble finding the right words.

'Well now, Mirabelle, as I said, it is good to meet you. You seem like a nice young lady and yet so very . . . so very . . .'

Mavis frowned. The two brothers looked at each other. Mavis tilted her head.

'. . . *Different*,' said Mavis, nodding slowly to herself, her brow wrinkling thoughtfully.

The Dibbles seemed terribly uneasy all of a sudden. Vernon tugged at his shirt collar. Byron cleared his throat nervously.

Lucius stopped preening his feathers and glared at them.

Enoch stepped forward. 'Aunt, would you like to be shown to your room?' he asked.

'Oh, but of course,' said Mavis, suddenly animated again. 'But first we must gather everyone together so that I might greet them all.' She patted down her dress and tucked some strands of hair behind her ears.

'Not everyone has arrived yet, Aunt,' said Odd.

If she had eyes, Mirabelle was certain Mavis would have been blinking in disbelief right now.

'Not arrived?' she spluttered. 'You mean I'm not the last one here?'

'Alas, no,' sighed Odd, trying his best to look sympathetic.

'It seems there was a mix up with the invitations,' said Enoch, looking pointedly at Odd.

Odd winked at Mirabelle.

'A mix up?' said Mavis, her voice rising in pitch, her nostrils flaring. 'But *everyone* was supposed to arrive before me. It's the done thing. It's only proper. Elegance above all else,' she said, shaking her head in disbelief. 'And nothing is more elegant than a proper entrance.'

Enoch bowed his head and gestured to the steps. 'If you would, Aunt.'

Mavis wriggled petulantly where she stood, fixed her hair again and then started regally up the steps. She stumbled for a moment on the first step and her boys rushed to her aid. She shrieked and flapped at them, but allowed them to take her by the arms and accompany her.

'Elegance above all else,' Odd whispered to Mirabelle.

'Winthropp,' Mavis called over her shoulder.

Her manservant took two large suitcases from the carriage. Despite not being much taller than Mirabelle or Odd, he seemed to have no difficulty carrying the luggage and followed Mavis nimbly up the steps. As he reached the top, he took a moment to look back. His two silver eyes fixed on Mirabelle for a moment, before he followed the Dibbles into the house. Mirabelle frowned.

'Always been a strange one, that Winthropp,' said Odd.

Enoch stood beside them, his hands clasped behind his back, watching as the Dibbles disappeared inside. He sighed. 'Mavis may well have one of her tantrums.' He looked at Odd. 'Perhaps you should go in and placate her.'

Odd looked panicked. 'Me? But, Uncle, I have so many tasks to accomplish, so many different things that demand my attention.'

Mirabelle grabbed him by the arm. 'Odd promised to help me with something, Enoch.'

Enoch looked unconvinced.

'That's right, Uncle, I did,' said Odd.

Enoch nodded. 'I see. Well, do what you must, Odd.' He started to walk into the house. 'But before the festivities commence you will be assigned to help Aunt Mavis. You are her favourite, after all. It wouldn't do to disappoint her.'

'Of course, Uncle,' Odd called after him. 'It would be my pleasure.'

Odd smiled at Mirabelle. 'Thank you. Now I need to run. I've—'

Mirabelle tightened her grip and he groaned.

'No, Mirabelle.'

'Please, Odd. It's been ages since I've seen him.'

'You saw him two days ago.'

'Just a quick visit.'

'But I have so many tasks to accomplish, so many—'

'Things that demand your attention. I know – that's what you keep telling everyone.'

Odd huffed like a sulky child. 'Get Winthropp to take you in the carriage.'

Mirabelle was not going to be deterred. 'A quick visit, Odd.' She squeezed his arm gently. 'He's your friend too.'

Odd looked forlorn now, and a little guilty. Mirabelle's heart leapt when she saw him draw a circle in the air with his little finger.

'A *quick* visit,' he said.

Mirabelle grinned.

They were outside Dr Ellenby's house in the village of Rookhaven in seconds. They could see a warm glow of orange light behind the curtains in his study.

'Maybe he's working,' Mirabelle said hopefully. Lucius cawed from his resting spot on her shoulder.

She knocked on the door. Before it opened, she frowned at Odd. 'You are coming in, aren't you?'

Odd pursed his lips and nodded. 'Of course.'

Mirabelle was about to say something else, but just then the door opened and Dr Davenport stood before them.

Doctor. He was hardly deserving of the title, Mirabelle thought. He was too young for a start. He had the fresh-faced look of someone just out of medical school. His hair was flattened with Brylcreem and parted down the middle. Mirabelle presumed he did it to make himself look older, but, in her opinion, it only made him look more like a schoolboy. He had his shirtsleeves rolled up and his top button undone. His brown tweed waistcoat was unbuttoned. To make matters worse, he was holding Dr Ellenby's pipe. Mirabelle knew his uncle had employed him to help with his workload while he was unwell, but in Mirabelle's eyes he was nothing like Dr Ellenby. He wasn't half as professional as his uncle, and she thought that using his uncle's pipe was more than a tad presumptuous.

She brushed past him into the hallway. He smiled nervously at her.

'I was putting my feet up,' he said.

Mirabelle looked at the pipe. 'Did you ask permission to use that?'

Dr Davenport opened and closed his mouth, looking first at Odd then at Mirabelle. He chuckled.

'I'm twenty-seven years of age, Mirabelle.'

'And I'm quite a bit older than that,' said Mirabelle. 'But you don't see me smoking my uncle's pipe without his permission.'

'Enoch doesn't smoke,' said Odd.

Mirabelle glared at him. She turned her attention back to Dr Davenport, feeling a mixture of delight and shame when she saw how nervous he looked. She tried to soften her tone.

'How is the patient today?'

Dr Davenport made a face, trying to look as agreeable and friendly as possible, keeping everything light.

'Good, good,' he said, a tad unconvincingly.

No one said anything for a moment. Mirabelle noticed that Odd was standing just inside the door as if he wanted to make a quick escape.

'Odd?'

He gestured at the study door. 'I'll wait in there. I'll talk to Paul.'

Paul? How very friendly you are, Odd, Mirabelle thought. She felt a quick pulse of anger, but she tried her best to smile. If she smiled, maybe that would help dispel the sudden awkwardness they all felt, that strange dark pressure in the air that seemed to push them further from each other even within the small space of the hallway.

Dr Davenport gestured towards the back of the house. 'He's in the sitting—'

'I know where he is,' said Mirabelle, already making her way down the hallway. 'You should put that pipe back where you got it from,' she called back.

Mirabelle pushed open the sitting-room door and closed it gently behind her. Dr Ellenby's armchair was in its customary position in front of the fireplace. There was a small fire crackling in the grate. Mirabelle felt the same nervous trepidation she always felt these days as she approached the chair. For a moment, she just stood there, frozen, aware of the darkness that cocooned the room, only broken by the light of the fire and the table lamp that glowed softly beside the armchair. She held her breath until she was fit to burst. She had no idea why. Even Lucius was silent, his head darting quietly back and forth as the firelight glinted off his good eye.

'If you're a burglar, I'd just like you to know that you're

not a very good one. Also, I don't really have much worth stealing.'

Mirabelle went towards the chair. She felt a sudden rush of relief. She didn't want to think about why that was. Lucius flew up and settled himself on top of a bookcase.

Dr Ellenby was sitting with a tartan blanket over his knees. He was wearing a woolly purple dressing gown, and there was a book open on his lap. He smiled at Mirabelle and she smiled in return, but she noticed the way the skin sagged around his eyes, making them look watery and larger, almost like those of a child. He was very pale, and his hair seemed finer than before, downy like a dandelion clock.

'How are you, Dr Ellenby?'

'All the better for seeing you, Mirabelle. Shouldn't you be at home preparing for the Configuration?'

Mirabelle shook her head. 'Almost everything is done. The guests have started to arrive. Odd is being kept busy.'

'How *is* Odd? I haven't seen him in a while.'

For a moment, Mirabelle thought about telling him that Odd was here with her, but the words wouldn't come. She smiled.

'He's complaining about having too much to do, but he's good.'

Dr Ellenby nodded. His eyes wandered to the fire. 'It must be very exciting to have so many members of the Family coming to Rookhaven.'

'I suppose it is,' said Mirabelle.

'And it happens so rarely. Once every one hundred years, so I've heard. I feel particularly blessed to be living in the time of one. It must be quite something to behold.'

'It's my first one,' said Mirabelle.

'And no doubt you'll have many more. Me, however—'

'Don't say it,' said Mirabelle, cutting him off.

Dr Ellenby sighed. 'It's the simple truth of being mortal.'

'I'm mortal too,' Mirabelle blurted out. She hadn't meant to say it, but there was something about the way Dr Ellenby looked that made her want to reach out to him, and now she'd spoken the words she couldn't take them back.

Dr Ellenby looked surprised. 'Really?'

'Yes. Enoch told me. He says it's because of my human

heritage. Those who are half human, half Family do age a lot slower than humans. An awful lot slower. But they still die eventually.'

She felt guilty as Dr Ellenby studied her face. She wondered now if it was somehow selfish of her to have revealed this to him, to make this conversation about her.

'And how did it make you feel when Enoch told you?'

Mirabelle thought back to the moment in the library. It had been just after her friend Jem had left. Enoch had told her about what she might expect as she got older. He had looked so troubled when he'd said the word 'mortal'. There had been sorrow in his eyes, though he had done his very best to buoy her spirits. She remembered the awful sinking feeling in the pit of her stomach, of fear, and sadness, but then there was also a strange relief, because if this were true it made her just like Jem, and if they were the same, then maybe . . .

She shook her head and lied. 'I don't know.'

Dr Ellenby nodded. 'I see.'

She turned her attention to the fire, holding her hands out to warm them. The only sound in the room was the crackle and spit of logs in the flames.

'What is it, Mirabelle? What's on your mind?'

Mirabelle knew that tone well. Warm, soft, sympathetic. It was impossible not to answer that voice.

'It's been six months,' she said.

'Since?'

Mirabelle turned to look at him. 'Since I last got a letter from Jem.'

Dr Ellenby nodded. 'I see.'

Mirabelle moved closer to the fire. 'I mean, is that normal, for people not to write? For your people, I mean. Odd says you're different with your customs.'

'This is true. We're different in many ways.' He fixed her with a look. 'We change. We grow up. Become different people.'

Mirabelle nodded. 'It's why she left, isn't it? She couldn't stay. She'd already changed.'

'She had her own path to follow. We all do. She grew up, and when humans do that they need to move on in life, to a new stage, become more independent, I suppose. They have to leave things behind.'

Mirabelle nodded. 'That's what Aunt Eliza said.'

Dr Ellenby looked at the book in his lap and tapped a finger against a page. Mirabelle noticed the faint tremor in his hand.

'I've been reading poetry. A lot of it is about change, moving on.' He took a sharp intake of breath through his nose. 'I find reading it refreshes me.' He tapped his chest with a fist. 'Makes me feel that little bit stronger.'

'Is he looking after you?'

Dr Ellenby looked slightly pained. 'Mirabelle.'

'Because if he isn't we can get somebody else. A better doctor. One that's older. I mean he looks barely out of short trousers. Is he even trained?'

'Paul is a very fine doctor. In many ways he's better than I was at his age.'

Mirabelle felt a sudden possessive fierceness take hold of her and she stepped in front of him. 'I don't believe that. I don't believe that for one minute, Dr Ellenby. Everyone in the village says you're the best.'

He took her hands in both of his and she knelt in front of him. His skin felt dry and papery, but he squeezed, and to Mirabelle it felt as if he were giving her all his strength.

'I've done what I can with the little life I've had, I suppose.'

'*Have* – the life you have,' said Mirabelle, squeezing his hands back.

Dr Ellenby chuckled, then he looked towards the mantelpiece, his eyes taking on a faraway look.

'Strange the directions in which life leads you. Destinations you hadn't planned for, the choices you make and where they take you. I was supposed to get married when I was younger. Her name was Rebecca. She was from Cornwall, and we were going to live there.'

Mirabelle was surprised by this revelation. 'Why didn't you get married?'

He lowered his eyes and looked at the book in his lap. 'Well, she became ill, you see. Very ill, and she . . .'

He waved a hand in the air to suggest nothing could have been done.

'I'm sorry,' said Mirabelle. They were both silent for a moment.

'I became a doctor after that. One doesn't have to be a genius to see why. Although it took me a while to take the plunge and commit to it.' His expression suddenly lightened. 'Did I ever tell you how I made my final decision?'

'No.'

'I spent a lot of time thinking about it, but I think I needed an extra little nudge. Then one night . . .'

He suddenly leaned sideways and winced, his hands tightening on Mirabelle's.

'You're in pain,' she said. 'You should rest. You can tell me next time.'

Dr Ellenby nodded, his face relaxed a little and he smiled encouragingly as Mirabelle stood up.

'Jem will write. She will. I'm sure of it. And you'll see her again, though she may not be the same, but neither will you be – that's just the way of it. You have your path and she has hers. Maybe one day they'll converge again. Who knows? But one thing I do know: things change, but they tend to change for the better. Trust me.'

Mirabelle bent down and hugged him. He hugged her back, and though he felt bird-boned and hollow she knew there was strength in him. There was always strength in him.

She stood up and smiled mischievously. He eyed her with amused suspicion.

'What?'

'I'll have something for you soon. A surprise.'

'What are you up to, Mirabelle of Rookhaven?'

'I don't have it with me right now, but I'll bring it with me next time.'

'A surprise, you say?'

'Yes.' Mirabelle couldn't help grinning when she thought about it. 'It's the best surprise ever. It's something I've been working on for a few months.'

'Hmm,' said Dr Ellenby, musing over this. 'Well then, I await my surprise with great anticipation, and I look forward to your next visit.'

'You are looking after him, aren't you?'

Mirabelle stood in the centre of the study, eyeing Dr Davenport. She'd found him laughing with Odd when she'd come back in. She didn't like him laughing. She thought there was something disrespectful about it.

'Yes, yes, of course,' said a flustered Dr Davenport.

'And he's getting plenty of rest and eating properly?'

Dr Davenport nodded rapidly, the way people do when they're trying their very best to placate somebody of whom they're frightened. Mirabelle felt a little twinge of guilt when she saw the way he was looking at her, but that was overshadowed by her urge to ensure that Dr Ellenby was getting the best care he possibly could.

Mirabelle spotted the pipe on the desk. Dr Davenport edged along the side of the desk in an effort to obscure her view.

'Can you please make sure to put his pipe back safely? He's had it a long time,' said Mirabelle, and Lucius, sitting on her shoulder, cawed at Davenport for good measure. Mirabelle turned to Odd.

'It's time to go. Unless you want to go in and see him?'

Odd swallowed and looked at Dr Davenport. 'He gets tired very easily. Isn't that right?'

'That's right,' said Dr Davenport. 'But a moment—'

'It's late. I wouldn't want to impose. Next time,' said Odd, a little too quickly.

He was already forming a portal in the air with his hand.

'Yes,' said Mirabelle. 'Next time.'

They both stepped into the portal and Dr Davenport waved goodbye.

In a blink, they were back outside the House of Rookhaven, and Mirabelle breathed in cool night air.

Odd looked at the ground. 'How is he?'

'He's good. A little tired maybe.' Mirabelle sighed. 'You should go and see him, Odd.'

'I will. I will,' he said, trying not to meet her eyes. There was a pause, and he smiled weakly. 'I should really get back to helping organise things.'

Mirabelle watched him open a portal and vanish. She sighed and shook her head.

'He's oh so busy, Lucius.'

Lucius cawed, almost sympathetically. Mirabelle absent-mindedly stroked him under his beak.

'Excuse me.'

Mirabelle wheeled round in surprise. Even Lucius gave a startled flutter.

There was a skinny dark-haired boy standing a few feet away from her on the driveway. He wore a stained white shirt under a charcoal-coloured tank top and had a tired, hunted look about him. There was a small satchel draped over his shoulder.

For a moment, Mirabelle was struck dumb. She had a sudden vivid image of Jem and Tom's arrival all those years ago. She remembered how vulnerable and frightened Jem had looked, standing there in her moth-eaten cardigan.

So when the boy jerked his head towards the house and asked, 'Is this the House of Rookhaven?' she smiled at him.

'Yes, yes, it is. Are you here for the Configuration?'

The boy nodded.

Mirabelle stepped towards him with her hand held out. 'I'm Mirabelle.'

The boy tentatively reached out and gave Mirabelle the limpest of handshakes. He took his hand back quickly, as if afraid he might be bitten.

Mirabelle tilted her head. 'And you are?'

'Billy. Billy Catchpole,' said the boy.

'Welcome, Billy.' Mirabelle gestured towards the house. 'Please, come in and make yourself at home.'

Billy blinked at her and clutched his tank top.

Mirabelle frowned in concern. 'Are you all right?'

He swallowed and nodded. Mirabelle went up the first step by way of encouragement. 'Come in. Where did you come from?'

'London,' said Billy.

He shuffled forward. Mirabelle gently encouraged him up the steps, noting how hunched he looked.

'How did you get here?' she asked.

'I walked,' he said.

Billy

They'd given Billy a map, but really there'd been no need. He didn't say this to Courtney or his henchmen. He didn't see any point in antagonising them, and in truth he didn't have any fight left in him after what they'd done to the Catchpoles.

He'd walked out of London and headed south. He took a cursory look at the map once he'd left the city behind, but as he made his way into the countryside he relied on his own senses to navigate. The air was filled with the scents and traces of beings not unlike himself who had travelled before him, almost always in the dead of night. It was clear to Billy that they were all converging on one point. There were dozens of these traces. Billy was surprised by the number. In all his years living in London, he'd only ever come across the Catchpoles and Meg. Beyond them there was only the occasional faint trace of a scent or a vibration on the air that suggested another of their kind had passed through, but no more than that. He supposed it made sense since all members of the Family preferred to stay out of sight of humans.

It took him four days to reach the forest and now he could see the shimmer of the barrier between the trees. It was not something humans could see, but to Billy it was like a thin veil, the lightest of shrouds separating two breaths. He passed through it and found himself on a chalk path leading towards a large house behind high stone walls.

Strange flowers bordered the path. Each one was over six feet tall, and as he made his way up the path they slowly unfurled their petals, sniffed the air, then bobbed their heads in greeting, recognising him instantly as someone who was entitled to be there. One of them stretched its neck towards him and Billy stopped for a moment and stroked its petals, while it cooed and nuzzled his face. He felt an overwhelming rush of emotion that he couldn't describe. He felt at home and yet desperately lost at the same time. Billy stayed there for a while, patting the flower.

He'd been halfway up the driveway to the house when his hackles became raised. There was no obvious threat he could see, but years spent in hiding meant he instinctively

crouched low in expectation. He knew why his instinct had kicked in as soon as he saw the portal appear and the boy and the girl step through it.

The boy was dressed in what looked like an old-fashioned school uniform. The girl wore a black dress. She was slim and pale, but there was something authoritative and dignified in the way she stood. She spoke to the boy for a few moments, then he disappeared into another portal.

Billy steeled himself, cradling the satchel tightly against his side, then stepped out from his cover and introduced himself.

The girl seemed friendly when she spoke, but even so Billy made sure to keep his wits about him. There was no telling what might happen now that he was out in the open. Magical barrier or no magical barrier, this had been the first time in years that Billy had spoken to anyone outside of the cellar, apart from Courtney and his thugs.

He followed Mirabelle up the steps and into the house.

The hallway was huge. Billy didn't like it. It felt worse than being outside.

Mirabelle beckoned. 'Come on, I'll introduce you.'

Billy pulled up for a moment and sniffed the air. There was a sudden scent, and then he heard sniggering. He wheeled round, trying to catch the source of the sound.

Someone tapped him on the shoulder, and the sniggering became louder.

'Gideon! Stop it,' said Mirabelle.

The scent was right in front of him now.

'Who's this, then?' said a disembodied voice.

Billy didn't think. His hand shot out and he grabbed at thin air, his fingers closing round something warm yet bony.

'Oi! Let go!' the voice roared.

A boy appeared right in front of him. He was grey scaled and skinny with one large eye in the middle of his forehead. He wrenched his arm out of Billy's grip.

'Manners,' the boy growled, rubbing his arm.

'You're the one who needs to learn manners, Gideon,' said Mirabelle.

Gideon had a small bone in one hand, and he stuck it in his mouth and gnawed at it, looking Billy up and down with distaste.

'Did you just crawl out from a ditch?'

Billy's cheeks flushed. Gideon moved around him, still looking him up and down. He moved in a jittery, twitchy way as if he bristled with energy and could barely contain himself.

'Billy came from London,' said Mirabelle.

'Same difference.' Gideon sniffed.

'He's here for the Configuration,' said Mirabelle more sternly. 'So you need to be a little more polite.'

Gideon snorted, working the bone between his teeth. Billy clenched a fist.

'What's in the bag?' Gideon asked, reaching for Billy's satchel.

'Nothing,' said Billy, taking a step back and holding the bag tightly.

Gideon's one eye gleamed and he grinned. 'Nothing? Looks more like something. Give it here.'

'Gideon,' Mirabelle warned. She put herself between Billy and Gideon. 'Forgive him,' she said to Billy. 'He's the youngest in the Family and he still has to learn his manners.'

'I've got manners,' said Gideon.

Mirabelle raised an eyebrow. 'Really?'

'Please thank you so kindly thank you very much excuse me.' Gideon bowed. 'See? Manners. Plenty of them.' He jerked his head at Billy. 'What about you? Have you got manners?'

Gideon spoke so rapidly it was hard for Billy to keep up with him. 'What?' he said.

'What? What? Don't you mean "excuse me"? That answers that, then.'

Billy opened his mouth to reply, but Gideon was on a roll.

'How old are you?'

'What?'

'Age. You know. How old?'

'I'm, I—'

'In years, I mean. Or centuries. Are you that old maybe? Mirabelle's not that old – neither am I.' He tapped his temple. 'I'm wise, though. I grew up fast, and I've got it all up here. Wise beyond my years, they say.'

'No one says that, Gideon,' said Mirabelle, rolling her eyes.

'So then, what about you, Billy? Tell us about yourself. We're all ears. Well, not all ears. Uncle Cedric is the only one we know who's all ears. He's *actually* all ears. You have to whisper really soft when he's around. Gets terrible headaches.'

Billy tried to answer, but nothing came out.

Gideon waved the bone at Billy. 'He needs teaching, Mirabelle. He needs teaching all about proper etiquette, and how to answer questions and—'

Mirabelle grabbed Gideon by the collar and started to push him towards the stairs. 'Go. Go now,' she said. 'Go and annoy somebody else. One of the Dibbles maybe, or Uncle Victor.'

Gideon's head twitched this way and that as he tried to look over Mirabelle's shoulder.

'Ask him where he's from. Ask him when he last changed his clothes. He looks like he could do with a bit of cleaning up. Ask him what it's like in the world outside.'

'Gideon!' Mirabelle roared.

Gideon vanished. There was the sound of feet running up the stairs, then they stopped for a moment, and Gideon shouted down, 'Ask him why he's so miserable-looking!'

The sound of Gideon's footsteps recommenced, and then faded away.

'Sorry about that,' said Mirabelle. 'He's a bit of a handful.'

'It's all right,' said Billy. Mirabelle's eyes alighted on his bag, and he instinctively pushed it behind his hip.

'Well, we should have a room for you, but first you must meet everybody else. I mean they're not all here. It's a few more days until the Configuration, and we're expecting more guests. Mavis is a bit put out because—'

'Everybody else?' asked Billy, annoyed by the hint of panic in his voice.

Mirabelle nodded. 'Yes, as many of the Family who could travel have come here.'

Mirabelle looked at him for a moment. Billy felt put on the spot, but he didn't know what to say. Instead, he nodded vigorously and mumbled something unintelligible, which he hoped might suffice for now.

'Are you all right, Billy?'

The genuine concern in Mirabelle's eyes took Billy by surprise.

'It's just that you must be tired after all your walking.'

Billy shook his head. 'No, I'm good at walking. I mean, I don't get tired easily.' He frowned. 'If at all. I just . . .'

Mirabelle took him by the arm. It took all his willpower not to pull away from her.

'Come and meet everyone, then,' she said.

Billy felt the overpowering urge to run as soon as they walked through the great double doors. He felt engulfed immediately by a hot, sweaty panic. The room was filled with dozens of chattering people, multicoloured spheres of light hovered in mid-air and its walls were covered in portraits that seemed to stretch on into infinity. Looking up made him feel nauseous and dizzy, so he kept his eyes trained on a midway point between himself and Mirabelle.

'This is the Room of Lights, but of course you know that,' said Mirabelle.

Billy nodded for show.

'You probably know some of the others already too.'

Something swooped down and positioned itself between Billy and Mirabelle. It was an enormous head with a sad-looking face, brown eyes, a tiny nose and a tiny mouth.

'Hello,' said the head.

The head was attached to an impossibly long and bendy neck that stretched from the shoulders of a man who was halfway across the room.

'Billy, this is Uncle Edgar,' Mirabelle said.

'Pleased to meet you,' said Uncle Edgar, his head bobbing gently back and forth as he examined Billy.

A huge bald man lumbered towards them. Billy could see his face was made of rock and he had tiny coal-black eyes. A nasally voice whined, 'Let me see, Siegfried. Let me see!'

The voice came from a jar strapped to the man's belt. The jar contained a gently roiling dark blue liquid surrounding a pair of eyes.

'Uncle Urg,' said Mirabelle, gesturing at the jar. 'And Siegfried,' she added looking up at the rock-like creature.

Siegfried gave a small bow, while Urg continued: 'Pleased to make your acquaintance . . .?'

'Billy. Billy Catchpole,' said Mirabelle.

'From?'

'Beyond, I should say, certainly not Rookhaven,' said a woman leaning over Billy's shoulder, while Edgar scrutinised his face with an interest that was now bordering on rude.

'This is Aunt Eliza,' said Mirabelle.

Eliza nodded and smiled at Billy. 'Welcome, Billy.'

'Maudlin, maybe, or Wyvern Street?' said Edgar to the group, looking Billy up and down as if he were some kind of laboratory specimen.

There was a sound like rocks grating against each other as Siegfried shook his head. 'Oh no, not Maudlin,' said Urg. 'I would know.'

Billy wiped his forehead. It was prickling with sweat, and he felt hemmed in. The air felt as if it were getting hotter. More people started to gravitate towards their group. A woman with a face covered with red lustrous hair, a small girl with gills pulsing along the sides of her neck. So many eyes on him now. Too many eyes. Billy took a step backwards.

Mirabelle placed a gentle hand on his shoulder and smiled at the assembled group.

'I think Billy needs to rest a little. He's had a long journey.'

None of them paid Mirabelle the slightest bit of attention and instead they just came closer. Billy looked from one to the other, panic fluttering in his chest, trying to slow his heartbeat. He saw the looks in their eyes. This was something beyond mere curiosity. *They knew. They knew he was different.* He was certain of it.

Someone complained about jostling. Someone else bumped into Edgar's head and he uttered a loud, 'Do you mind?' People started to babble. Billy felt the hairs stand up on his neck. He sensed an electric charge in the air. Something was coming. He could feel it. Billy turned to his right, already crouching. Mirabelle was asking him a question, but he barely registered it, so strong was the rushing sensation he felt.

He saw the portal form inches in front of him. The boy he'd seen earlier outside the house stepped through it with his head down. He was looking at a large egg he held between his hands. Billy did what came instinctively just as the boy looked up.

He punched him.

The force of the punch was enough to knock the boy off his feet and send him skidding across the floor. There was a collective gasp from everyone present, a stunned pause, then a torrent of voices, like water greedily rushing in after the breaking of a dam.

Eliza helped the boy up. He was covered in egg yolk and broken shell. He shook his head in an effort to clear it. He looked dazed. Billy immediately felt guilty as Mirabelle turned to him, her lips pursed.

'Why did you do that?' she asked.

Billy couldn't explain. How could he? He wanted to, but he was afraid to say anything at all in case he revealed his true purpose.

Mirabelle went to the boy and took one arm while Eliza took the other. They half carried him back towards where Billy stood, while dozens of eyes looked on accusingly.

'I think you need to apologise to Odd,' said Mirabelle.

Billy looked at him. Odd's eyes were foggy as he scrunched up his forehead and tried to focus on Billy. Mirabelle and Eliza slowly let go of his arms.

Mirabelle gave Billy a pointed look. He licked his lips, keenly aware that all eyes were still on him and that the whole room had gone unnaturally quiet.

'I'm suh . . . I'm sorry I hit you,' he said.

Odd nodded. 'Apology accepted.' He smiled, then his right leg seemed to go out from under him, but Mirabelle caught him just in time.

Billy looked at Mirabelle. 'It was a misunderstanding.'

Mirabelle sighed, but she seemed to relax and accept his apology.

'Well, that was certainly entertaining,' said Edgar. He pulled his head back in towards his body, and the rest of the crowd seemed to take that as their signal to disperse.

Billy could hear Uncle Urg's voice as Siegfried shambled away.

'Thornwood, perhaps. Lovely house, lovely people. Although maybe not. He seems a little uncouth to be from there. Also, there are very few ways in there. Quite exclusive. Not like here.'

Siegfried shrugged, raising a small cloud of dust around his shoulders.

'They're all a bit overexcited because of the Configuration,' said Mirabelle.

'Nosy too,' said Eliza, letting go of Odd's arm. Billy took note of how elegant she looked in her shimmering purple gown with her hair piled up in waves on her head, but he also caught sight of the gentle rippling of her skin.

'Billy's here for the Configuration,' said Mirabelle to Odd.

'Not just to punch people, then? Well, that's encouraging,' said Odd.

Billy looked at the floor. He had to remind himself that he was here to do something important, not draw attention to himself, and that these people were not out to hunt him. These weren't the streets of London. He felt even more guilty for hitting Odd when Odd was generous enough to smile at him.

'I should get cleaned up,' said Odd, wiping sticky egg yolk from his hands.

'And we need to get you to your room,' Mirabelle said to Billy.

Billy sensed a presence to his left. The rest of the Family members had dispersed around the room, but one lone figure was standing just a few feet away from him. He was short and wearing a cowl, beneath which Billy saw eyes burning like small silver stars. Try as he might, he couldn't make out any more of the figure's face within the darkness of the hood.

Odd looked at Billy. 'This is Winthropp. Like you, he's not the most talkative type. I suspect the two of you will get on like a house on fire.'

Winthropp looked at Billy, tilting his head slightly, as if curious. Then he turned slowly and walked away. Billy's skin crawled. Being stared at by members of the Family had made him feel as if he were suffocating. Being stared at by Winthropp on the other hand made him feel cold and exposed.

Mirabelle led Billy upstairs towards the top of the house. She told him that many of the rooms were already occupied for the Great Configuration. Billy nodded as if he understood everything she said.

The room she brought him to was grey and cramped, with a single bed, a wash basin and a jug on a dresser. The heavy drapes were drawn, but Billy could see everything as if it were full daylight. Mirabelle lit a single candle on the dresser for him.

'So, this is yours for the duration,' said Mirabelle.

Billy nodded.

'You can come down any time you like.'

Billy nodded.

'You don't say very much, do you?'

Billy shook his head.

Mirabelle laughed, then put a hand to her mouth in contrition. 'I'm sorry. That was rude of me.'

Billy felt his cheeks burn slightly.

'Where are you really from, Billy?'

Billy remembered what Thorne had drilled into him.

'The Ether,' he said, a little too quickly.

'I know that – we're all from . . .' Mirabelle winced. 'Well, most of us come from there, but which gateway? Stokely? Maudlin? Enoch tells me that there's a cave somewhere. Not many have come from there. More come from here.' Mirabelle rubbed the jamb of the door and smiled. 'But then again Rookhaven is somewhere special.'

Billy thought about the cellar and the Catchpoles, and how everything before that was just a blank. He thought about telling her everything right then and there because Mirabelle seemed nice, but then he felt the weight of the thing in his satchel, and he remembered Meg's frightened eyes and what he was here for, and he remembered the sanctuary name he'd been given.

'Osric,' he mumbled.

Thorne had told him the name of what he called a 'minor house'. Billy didn't know what that meant, but Thorne had told him no one would ask too many questions about such a place.

Mirabelle nodded in satisfaction. 'I don't know much about Osric. Maybe you could tell me.'

She clearly saw the panicked look on his face because then she said, 'Sorry. I shouldn't be nosy. It's rude.' Billy felt relieved as she turned to go, but then she looked back, and frowned at him.

'Why did you hit Odd?'

Billy swallowed. 'I don't know . . . I . . .'

'You're not that used to people, are you?'

Her eyes locked with his. Billy didn't know what to say. Mirabelle gave a little nod and then left, closing the door behind her.

Billy looked around the small grey room. He eyed the bed, then went to the dresser and placed his satchel on it. He looked furtively at the door before putting his hand into the satchel and taking out the orb. He placed it on the dresser and traced the runes with a finger while the reflected candlelight flickered warm and gold along its silver surface. His lips moved as he went through the instructions in his head.

Billy looked at the bed again. He went towards it, pressed a hand gingerly against the mattress, then lay on it.

He remembered seeing a man in the window of a furniture shop in London trying out a bed once. He'd lain on the bed with his hands behind his head while the shop assistant spoke to him.

Billy tried to lie with his hands behind his head. It didn't feel right, so he lay there rigid with his arms down by his sides. He turned, first one way then the other. He couldn't escape the feeling that he was sinking through the mattress. None of this felt right so he eventually got off the bed and just lay on the wooden floor.

He looked up at the ceiling, its beams knotted and whorled, candlelight rendering the surface into a series of fluid shapes and shadows. He tried to think about what he had been promised as reward for a successful mission. A home, somewhere above ground for himself and Meg. A place they could feel safe. Yet even if that dream could be realised, which was uncertain, there was still a gnawing feeling in his heart.

The dreadful sense that he and Meg would still be outcasts.

Mirabelle

As Mirabelle made her way down into the depths of the house, she thought about Billy. He looked so wary. She wondered what it was that had made him so. Part of her wasn't surprised when he'd lashed out at Odd. He seemed so on edge, as if he were being pursued by someone. Again, she was reminded of Jem and Tom when they'd first arrived, especially Jem's nervous demeanour.

There was something else too, but she couldn't put her finger on it, until the word popped unbidden into her head.

Different.

It was a word she'd heard a lot in recent weeks. When the first guests had arrived, and she'd been introduced, she'd heard it whispered among them. As grateful as they were (or so they kept telling her) for her vanquishing of the Malice, there were still those odd suspicious glances, the conspiratorial murmurs whenever she entered a room. She'd voiced her annoyance to Odd, but he'd simply waved it away as if it were nothing.

She took a deep breath and put it to the back of her mind. For now, she had more important matters at hand. She stood before the door to Piglet's room.

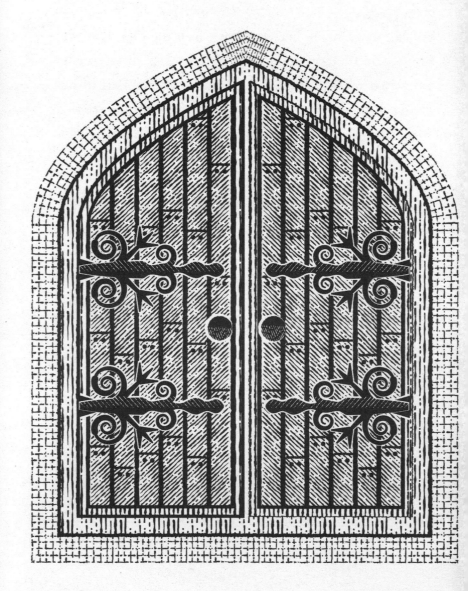

Piglet

Piglet is listening to the voices. He likes to listen.

So many voices, and all so different. Some he knows, some he doesn't. All of them seem giddy with anticipation, and there is magic in the air, as if something wonderful is approaching. Piglet knows this feeling. He has sensed it many times, has heard voices speak of it with excitement before. It is old magic, powerful, mysterious. Magic as old as Piglet.

Perhaps even older.

The voices seem happy, and the air feels filled with light and it makes Piglet happy too.

Happy. Yes. Piglet likes being happy.

He is even happier when the door opens and Mirabelle enters his room. He likes the way she talks to him, using her mouth to form words. Piglet tilts his head and examines the way she does it. It seems slow to him, and delightful, and funny. He likes being talked to in this way, but he can't imagine doing it himself. It just seems to take so long to express so few thoughts.

And then Mirabelle is wagging her finger at him and her forehead is wrinkling, and she looks stern as she tells him the same thing she's been telling him for months.

Piglet nods. He is very grave now. Very attentive.

Except there is an owl hooting outside and he hears it and the night air ripples through its feathers and for a moment

Piglet wishes he was with the owl.

And there is something else. He sensed it when the door opened. A new scent. A smell. Strong. A heady mixture of fear, sadness and desperation. Piglet frowns. This is new. This is very new, and yet also familiar. Oddly familiar. Almost like . . .

Mirabelle is shouting now. Piglet tries to pay attention again. He—

'. . . must pay attention.'

That's what she says with her words. Piglet smiles. He nods. He listens.

But even at the back of his mind he still wonders about that small, sad new presence.

A tiny speck of darkness amidst all the light.

Billy

Billy watched the sun come up through his bedroom window.

He'd spent the night sitting on the edge of his bed listening to the inhabitants of the house wandering around, chatting among themselves. He'd heard some dreadful warbling at one point that he presumed was someone's attempt at singing. The pitch was high and reedy, so he thought the most likely culprit was that uncle in the jar he'd met in the Room of Lights. At one point he'd heard something else – a distant roar – and he could have sworn that for just one moment all activity in the house had stopped, as if everyone were listening to the same thing. He tensed and found himself eyeing the door as if something might burst through it at any moment. The bustle and noise returned after a pause, but there was no mistaking the sense that everyone had taken a little intake of breath. Things became a bit more animated after midnight, but with the advent of sunrise there had been a definite decrease in activity.

Billy reached into the satchel and took out the stone pendant Thorne had given him. He was under strict instructions to wear it if he had to go out in daylight.

'Your type needs to blend in, boy. You'll need to pass

yourself off as one of them, unable to go out in the light,' Thorne had snarled.

Billy didn't like the look in the man's eyes, the contempt that burned there, bordering on rage. He thought about Meg then and felt a flicker of rage himself. Thorne had better be keeping her safe. He clenched the pendant tightly and looked at it. It was roughly carved, its symbols portraying a moon and a sun separated by a sword. A scraggly piece of twine was looped through it.

Billy laid the necklace on the bed.

There was a gentle tapping on the door. Billy froze.

The tapping came again and a timid voice said: 'Can I come in?'

Before he could reply, a small girl walked right through the locked door. Billy sprang to his feet, clutching his satchel to his chest, feeling the weight of the object inside it.

The girl had gold ringlets and wore a blue-and-white checked pinafore. She smiled up at him, but Billy could see the tiniest glitter of malice in her eyes.

'Hello,' she said. 'I'm Daisy. Why are you awake?'

'Why are *you* awake?' Billy snapped.

'We're nosy,' said a voice to his right.

Billy whirled round to see the head of an identical-looking girl poking through the bedroom wall.

'That's Dotty, my sister,' said Daisy.

'Pleased to meet you,' said Dotty, easing the rest of her body through the wall and into the bedroom. She was the mirror image of Daisy, right down to her ringlets and dress.

The two girls advanced on him. Billy held his satchel tighter.

'What's your name?' asked Dotty, her eyes guileless.

'Billy. What's yours?'

'Billy? That's a nice solid ordinary name, isn't it?' said Daisy, flashing him a smile.

Billy didn't know what to say.

Daisy did a mock curtsy. 'We're so very pleased to meet you, Billy.'

Billy nodded at the door. 'Well, you can go now.'

Daisy burst out laughing, and Billy felt a quick little ripple of anger at the sound.

'That's not very nice now, is it? We're only trying to make conversation,' said Dotty.

The door opened suddenly, and Mirabelle stood there, glaring at the twins.

'You two. I knew you were up to no good. Why aren't you sleeping?' she said.

'How could we sleep when we have an interesting new visitor?' said Daisy haughtily.

Mirabelle stepped into the room and shook her head. 'I'm sorry about these two, Billy. They're just rude.'

Daisy pursed her lips and put her hands on her hips. 'Rude?' she shrieked.

'He is, though, isn't he?' said a voice by the door. 'Interesting.'

Billy caught the whiff of his scent right before the one-eyed boy materialised. He leaned against the jamb, his arms folded, his one eye bright with mischief as he grinned.

Mirabelle groaned. 'Gideon, not you as well.'

Gideon sauntered into the room, looking Billy up and down.

Billy clenched his jaw and squeezed the satchel to his chest.

Gideon started to circle him. Mirabelle growled a warning, but Gideon ignored her, continuing to eye Billy. Billy glared back at him. If anyone was deserving of a punch, it was this boy now. He would gladly punch him. As hard as he could.

He was aware that Daisy was now looking at him with suspicion too.

'There's something funny about you. Where are you from again?' she said.

Billy felt another surge of anger, but quelled it, and instead looked to Mirabelle for help. He could see the apology in her eyes.

'Gideon, Daisy, just leave him alone. He's a guest.'

Gideon sniffed Billy's hair. 'Oh, I'd say he's much more than that. He's—'

Billy had had enough. He swung the satchel one handed at Gideon, missing his head by inches as Gideon ducked and vanished in the same instant.

Billy growled and swung his arm again, but something kicked his legs out from under him, and he was aware of Mirabelle shouting, 'Gideon!' and then his satchel was ripped from his hands. Panic enveloped Billy as he scrabbled forward and snatched at the satchel hovering just above his head. It was snapped out of his reach and Gideon reappeared close to the window. He started to undo the straps.

'There must be something very important in here if you're so eager to want it back. I wonder what it—'

Billy launched himself across the room, fully intending to grab the satchel and do as much damage to Gideon as he could in the process. Gideon's eye widened, and he side-stepped just as Billy grabbed the bag, clutching it to his chest like a rugby player making a try.

Billy saw Gideon blink in astonishment as he hurtled past him, and with a crushing sense of doom knew his momentum was too much. He couldn't stop himself.

Billy went right through the curtain and out of the window. Wood and glass exploded around him. He flipped over, still holding the bag. His right side hit the sharp edge of some guttering. He gasped in pain, unable to react in time as his head now hit a slate, shattering it. He slid down the roof, the sunlight flaring in his eyes as he scrabbled for purchase.

Fury took him now, hot and focused. He saw everything

with a terrible angry clarity. Instinct kicked in as he grabbed the brass moulding of a turret and swung himself round to give himself direction. He flipped over, hit the mercifully sturdy line of some ancient guttering, and then tumbled once, twice, before the ground came hurtling towards him.

He had a fleeting thought. This wouldn't be like when he'd been captured in London. This time he was ready.

Billy landed on his feet on the gravel, crouching to cushion his fall. A sharp pain juddered up his right side, but he snarled in an effort to quell it.

He had the satchel in one hand. He could feel the bulge underneath the canvas. Relief washed over him. He still had it. It was safe.

Billy straightened up. He ran his hands over his body. He had no cuts and bruises he could see, although there was a low burning sensation in his right side. He hoped that would be gone soon.

He'd landed outside the front door of the house. The door opened and Mirabelle stood there, looking shocked. She was holding something in her hand. She came towards him.

Then Billy remembered something.

The morning sun was blazing.

His hand went to his neck in a blind panic. But, of course, there was nothing there. He'd left it on the bed.

Mirabelle stood before him, holding up the stone pendant.

Mirabelle

Mirabelle looked at the pendant she'd put on Enoch's desk. Enoch picked it up and felt the weight of it in the palm of his hand. He wrinkled his nose.

'Rather crude craftsmanship.'

Billy sat across from him, his hands over the satchel in his lap, his head bowed. Eliza was to Enoch's left, while Aunt Mavis sat on Enoch's right.

The whole house had been woken by the shrieking of the twins. Mavis had been one of the first on the scene to hear the twins breathlessly recount the story of the boy falling out of the window. Several more Family members had gathered in the hallway to observe the commotion. They whispered among themselves about Billy, and Mirabelle noticed how warily some of them looked at her. Mirabelle saw Mavis conferring with Winthropp, and there was a look of obvious distaste on her face when Mirabelle had shepherded Billy past her and the other curious Family members.

Mavis had insisted on being here because she maintained it was her right as a senior member of the Family. Mirabelle reckoned it was just out of sheer nosiness. She also knew that Enoch had given in to Mavis's demand purely so he wouldn't have to listen to her complaining about not being allowed in. Although, judging from the pained look on his face, Mirabelle could tell he was already beginning to regret his decision.

Meanwhile, Winthropp sat cross-legged on a low chair in the corner, flipping through the pages of a small leatherbound notebook. For some reason, Mavis had requested that he be present also. Occasionally he would look over in their direction. Mirabelle tried to avoid his gaze, but even when she wasn't looking at him she could feel the oppressive weight of those silver eyes set in that hooded darkness.

Mirabelle stood beside Billy. She'd felt almost duty-bound to accompany him once the summons had come from Enoch. The stricken look on his face when she'd shown him the pendant had made her feel even more sorry for him. Daisy had, of course, been first to run to Enoch to tell him about 'the boy who didn't burn'. Her mixture of horror and delight disgusted Mirabelle and made her even more determined to stand up for him.

'Billy? That's your real name, is it?' asked Enoch.

Billy nodded, unwilling to lift his head.

'Not the talkative type, I see,' said Enoch.

Mavis rapped the table with a knuckle. 'Well, he'd better start talking,' she said. 'I think it's rather vulgar of someone to come here under false pretences.'

Mirabelle bristled at this. 'He can't be here *under false pretences* if he made his way through the Glamour and safely along the Path of Flowers now, can he? He entered through the Glamour unobstructed – that means he's of the Family.'

Mavis wiggled her shoulders and looked indignant. 'Well now, I should think—'

She was silenced by Enoch. 'Mavis, please. No one is on trial here.'

Mavis pursed her lips and folded her arms.

Eliza leaned forward. 'Where are you from, Billy?'

Billy looked up shiftily. 'London, Osric,' he said quietly.

There was the sound of the riffling of pages as Winthropp nonchalantly played with his notebook. Everyone turned to him for a moment, but he ignored them. Mirabelle felt a twinge of irritation at his behaviour.

Enoch appraised Billy with his dark eyes. 'You're sure

you didn't come from somewhere else?'

'Did you come from the Ether?' Eliza asked gently.

Billy looked anguished for a second.

Mavis snorted and flapped a dismissive hand. 'Him? The Ether?'

Mirabelle glared at her.

'Mavis, if you could just keep quiet for a moment,' said Enoch.

But Mavis wasn't one to keep quiet. Mirabelle felt her cheeks get hotter the more Mavis spoke.

'I mean, look at him. Even the way he carries himself. No style, no grace. Certainly not of the Ether. I mean, let's face it, he didn't burn, but he managed to gain access through the Glamour. That can only mean one thing.' She flicked her hand at Mirabelle. 'I mean *she* doesn't burn, and we all know why *that* is, don't we?'

Eliza caught Mirabelle's eye, seeing the flash of irritation before anyone else. She tried to speak, but Mirabelle cut her off.

'Tell me, Aunt Mavis, why *is* that?' asked Mirabelle.

Mavis gave a shrug. 'We all know. It's common knowledge, after all.'

Mirabelle gave a simpering smile. 'Common knowledge or not, I'd like to hear what you mean.'

Mavis wagged a finger. 'Now, I don't mean to be ungrateful. I mean we all are very grateful indeed, from Rookhaven to beyond. Your legend has spread far and wide—'

Enoch tried to intervene. 'Mavis, if you could just—'

'But facts are facts,' said Mavis, who was warming to her theme now. 'You are not strictly of the Family. I mean, you didn't come from the Ether, and neither did this boy. His heritage is much like yours, I presume. Half human, which leaves him protected from sunlight. He is – and I hesitate to use the word . . .'

'Somehow I don't think you do,' muttered Eliza.

'He is one of the *Misbegotten*,' Mavis said, looking nauseous and shuddering for dramatic effect.

Enoch closed his eyes and shook his head. Eliza half turned away as if in disgust. Mavis sat back in her chair and released a self-satisfied exhalation. Billy looked at his hands in his lap.

'You'll have to explain that word to me, Aunt. I don't think I've ever heard it before,' Mirabelle growled.

Mavis seemed oblivious to her growing anger. 'Well, you should have.' She jerked her head towards Enoch. 'I would have thought your guardian would have seen to your education on that matter.'

Enoch glowered at her. 'That's not a word we use in this house, Mavis.'

Mavis looked aghast. 'Well, you *should*.' She jabbed her finger against the table. 'Family and Misbegotten, separate and distinct. This was established at the Conclave in 1532 in Wyvern. I was there.' She looked at Mirabelle and held her hands up. 'As I said, dear, I don't mean to seem ungrateful for all you've accomplished, but your education matters and you should be treated according to your proper position. I'd really rather see a situation where you were made aware of the *difference* so that you can carry on your life accordingly, conscious of your true status in civil society.'

'Oh, do please be quiet for once, you stupid, silly, ignorant woman,' Eliza said, sighing.

Mavis looked gobsmacked. 'What, w-w . . .' she stammered.

Eliza leaned towards her, enunciating her words slowly and calmly. 'I said, *be quiet*.'

A pair of eyes suddenly appeared on Mavis's face, like the twin corpses of tiny fish bobbing to the surface of a fishbowl. She looked aghast at Enoch. Both her eyes blinked rapidly for a moment, then disappeared. 'She can't talk to me like that,' she said, in the aggrieved foghorn tone of one who has been too conceited and sure of getting her own way for far too long.

Mirabelle caught movement out of the corner of her eye while the adults bickered among themselves. Winthropp had put away his notebook and was slowly leaning his elbows on his thighs, clawed hands clasped together as he turned his silver orbs on her and Billy, watching them with obvious fascination.

Billy was still looking at the floor but Mirabelle stared defiantly back at Winthropp, her nostrils flaring. Unable to challenge him for any obvious reason, she took her anger and directed it towards the others.

'*Misbegotten* . . . Uncle, what does that *mean*?'

Now Mavis folded her arms and waited for Enoch's response. He seemed reluctant to talk about the subject, making a hesitant attempt to start.

'It is . . . a term . . .'

'It means you're half human and therefore not a *proper* member of the Family.' Mavis nodded in Billy's direction and sniffed haughtily. 'Him too.'

Billy looked up at this, then quickly lowered his eyes again.

'So I'm . . . we are considered inferior in some way?' said Mirabelle.

'If you like, yes,' said Mavis.

Mirabelle looked at Enoch and Eliza. 'And how widespread is this attitude among members of the Family?'

'Within the walls of Rookhaven you are our Mirabelle. You are Family,' said Eliza fiercely.

'Within,' said Mirabelle flatly. 'But beyond?'

Enoch couldn't seem to look her in the eye. 'Beyond you would not be considered a fully fledged member of the Family.'

'Which is outrageous!' said Eliza, slamming her hand down on the table.

Mavis turned her mouth down in a gesture of smug dismissal. Mirabelle stared at her.

'But you are *grateful* for what I did,' said Mirabelle.

'Oh, but of course, my dear child,' said Mavis.

'It almost makes me wish I hadn't done it.'

Mavis ignored the comment and addressed the room

without looking at anyone. 'There is still the matter of confirming this boy's heritage.'

Enoch shook his head. 'I don't think—'

Mavis gave a high-pitched command: 'Winthropp!'

Winthropp stood up from his chair and made his way towards Billy and Mirabelle.

'Dear Winthropp, if you would be so kind,' said Mavis in that unctuous, simpering tone of hers.

Winthropp took a step closer to Mirabelle. She tensed and was shocked when he sniffed the air a few inches from her. He made his way towards Billy and sniffed around him too. Then Winthropp straightened up and looked at Mavis.

'Well?' said Mavis.

Winthropp merely nodded, then went back to the chair.

Mavis grinned at Enoch and Eliza. 'You see? Winthropp has always had the unerring ability to detect one of the Misbegotten. It has been proven time and time again. Now, to conclude, we must decide what to do with the boy.'

'We?' said Enoch.

'Yes, naturally.'

'We,' said Enoch drily, exchanging a look with Eliza. Eliza smiled thinly. Enoch turned back to Mavis. 'Who are you exactly?'

Mavis looked startled. 'Why, I am Mavis Dibble,' she spluttered indignantly.

'Of?' said Eliza.

'*Of*? What do you mean *of*?'

Mirabelle felt a delicious twinge of delight at Mavis's increasing discomfort. 'She means of where, Aunt. *Where* did you come from?'

'Are you of Rookhaven?' said Enoch, his tone so mild and even that Mirabelle felt like applauding him.

'Why no, I am of Montforth,' said Mavis, her cheeks now splashed with a high pink colour.

'A lovely place,' said Enoch. 'Dark, but lovely.'

'By the sea, if I remember correctly, grey and salty, buffeted by the wind and rain,' said Eliza.

'How very poetic,' said Enoch.

'Why, thank you,' said Eliza.

Mavis's face was reddening now, and she was wobbling with rage.

'And this is Rookhaven,' said Mirabelle, trying not to laugh.

'Precisely,' said Enoch.

'Rookhaven, not Montforth,' said Eliza.

'And *we* are of Rookhaven,' said Mirabelle.

Enoch looked at Mirabelle. 'Those called *Misbegotten* have always been welcome here.'

All eyes turned to Mavis now. She looked ready to explode.

Enoch's eyes glittered.

'The boy stays,' he said.

There was some mild squealing from Mavis after Enoch made his pronouncement. Winthropp had to coax her from the room as she continued protesting.

Mirabelle was glad to see the back of both of them. Enoch asked her to escort Billy back to his room, but Eliza interrupted and said she'd be happy to do it. She nodded at Mirabelle as she left with Billy, and Mirabelle was grateful for her understanding; Eliza knew that she wanted to talk to Enoch.

As they sat across from each other, Enoch laced his fingers together.

'You have questions, Mirabelle.'

Mirabelle sighed. The look she gave him was steady and unwavering. 'It seems I always have questions, Uncle. Maybe you could answer them honestly this time.'

Billy

Billy kept facing ahead as he and Eliza made their way upstairs. He could feel her eyes on him.

'Why are you here, Billy Catchpole?'

Billy shook his head. 'I . . . I had nowhere else to go.'

'Really?'

He didn't like the way she let the word just hang in the air.

'I don't have a home,' he said, 'and I'm always on the move, and I'd heard about Rookhaven, and the Great Configuration, and it just sounded . . .'

They'd reached the landing. Eliza stopped, and Billy had no choice but to stand there while she appraised him. The silence was worse than being asked questions. He didn't know where to look.

'Sounded . . . ?'

Billy resisted the urge to wipe sweat from his forehead. 'Welcoming,' he said. And this was partially true, but only because he thought of how hospitable Mirabelle had been.

Eliza nodded and seemed content with his response, for now.

'What will happen to me?' Billy asked.

Eliza frowned. 'What do you mean?'

'You know, shouldn't I be . . .?'

Billy couldn't finish the sentence. Eliza put a hand on his shoulder and halted their progress.

'Do you really expect us to send you away?'

Billy couldn't look her in the eye. 'I don't know . . . I mean, I'm not . . .' He stared hard at the floor.

'You're welcome here, Billy. We learned a long time ago in Rookhaven that you don't just turn people away.' Eliza stretched her arm out. 'Isn't that right, Gideon?'

Eliza's arm fell away as the thousands of spiders that formed it suddenly spread out and spun in lines around something rounded and invisible that seemed to hang in mid-air. Billy's hackles rose as he saw them form the shape of a familiar head with one eye.

'Spying again?' said Eliza.

'I don't spy,' said Gideon, an invisible hand brushing at the spiders on his face. Eliza wagged a finger at him.

'I think you have an apology to make,' said Eliza.

Gideon materialised beside them. The spiders flowed off his face and reformed as Eliza's arm in a gentle liquid movement that Billy found hypnotic.

'What for?' Gideon grunted.

'For your lack of hospitality,' said Eliza.

Gideon's eye flicked to Billy. He sighed. 'Sorry,' he said, looking at the floor.

'Properly,' said Eliza.

An exasperated Gideon straightened up. 'I'm sorry for what I did.'

'And it won't happen again,' said Eliza.

'And it won't happen again,' said Gideon, rolling his eye.

'Good, very good,' said Eliza.

'Is it true you're like Mirabelle?' said Gideon.

Billy didn't know what to say in response.

'That you're half human?'

'How do you know this?' snapped Eliza. 'Were you in the room the whole time?'

Gideon grinned and twitched. 'No. Yes. Not the whole time. Is it true, though?'

Eliza took Billy gently by the elbow. 'Go and entertain yourself some other way, Gideon,' she said over her shoulder.

She leaned down towards Billy. 'He's not a bad sort, really, but he does need to learn to control his impulses a little.'

She led Billy back to his room. Billy knew he wasn't out of the woods yet, otherwise she wouldn't have escorted him in the first place. His suspicions were confirmed when they reached his room and she said, 'Enoch may need to question you further.' She looked at him, as if trying to gauge his reaction. Billy tried his best to look her straight in the eye. He could hear the ticking of a clock downstairs, and the gentle fizzing of spiders as she tilted her head. The moment seemed to last forever.

'He'll probably talk to you again soon. But I'm sure you've nothing to hide. Mirabelle is a fine judge of character,' said Eliza. 'For now, I suggest you make yourself at home.'

She smiled, and Billy sighed inwardly with relief as she bade him goodbye and walked away.

Billy closed the door behind him and listened for a moment as Eliza's steps receded. Then he put his satchel on the bedspread and knelt down to reach under the bed. He grabbed the blanket and pulled it out. He unwrapped it to find the orb was still there. Relieved, he wrapped it up again and shoved it back under the bed.

The window had already been boarded up, but even the gloom wouldn't stop him.

Billy sat cross-legged on the bed, reached into the

satchel and took out his precious copy of *Treasure Island*. Almost hungry for it, he started to read.

Odd

Odd sat on a hill and watched the moon rise over a small fishing village.

He'd ventured out on the pretence of picking something up for the Configuration. To be honest, Odd just wanted to get out of the house for a while. There was too much frenetic activity going on for his liking, and he felt as if he were being pulled in a thousand different directions as his relatives asked him for this, that and the other for the duration of their stay.

He just needed some fresh air and space – that was all.

He closed his eyes and listened to the soft thud and clink of boats and mooring ropes in the night, the waft of air coming from the water, the gentle lapping of the sea at the edge of the harbour walls.

Tobacco.

The word popped uninvited into his head. It seemed to be happening quite a bit lately. Certain words would pop into his head. Sometimes there were whole sentences.

Get Marcus some tobacco.

Odd opened his eyes and

sighed. Yes, he supposed he could do that. It would be a nice thing to do while the doctor was resting up. A tin of his favourite tobacco sitting there waiting for him when he was fully recovered.

Resting up. That's how Odd liked to refer to it. It seemed reasonable to him. Very soon Marcus would surely be up and about again, full of vim and vigour, and tending to his patients just like before.

Resting up.

'He's being well looked after,' said Odd to himself.

He stood up swiftly and stretched his legs. Time to move on, he supposed. He felt a little restless, and any time he felt like that he always moved on. He looked at the dark water that lay in front of him, the way the moonlight shimmered and rippled softly on the liquid black surface. He breathed in the night air in an effort to centre himself.

And you should go visit him.

'Yes, yes, soon,' Odd snapped at the voice in his head.

He made a circular motion with his index finger and thought about the main hall in the House of Rookhaven. He stepped through the portal.

He arrived in the hallway, relieved to find it was empty. Then someone said, 'Pssst,' from above, and he rolled his eyes and looked up to see Gideon hanging by his ankles from the chandelier.

'She knows,' said Gideon.

Gideon filled him in on all the details of the meeting, and the revelations about the Misbegotten. Odd was genuinely surprised about the boy. Billy didn't seem like the devious sort to him. He felt a creeping unease when Gideon told him how angry Mirabelle had been when she'd discovered, not only about the status of the Misbegotten, but the fact that it had been kept from her.

It's Mirabelle, he thought. *Of course she'll want to do something rebellious in response.*

Gideon was still blathering away when Odd caught sight of Mavis and her sons approaching. He immediately opened a portal and stepped through it, ignoring Gideon's offended squawk.

He arrived at the door of his room to find Mirabelle waiting for him. She had a defiant look in her eyes. Odd shook his head. He knew what was coming next.

'We do it tonight,' she said.

'That wasn't the plan,' said Odd. 'We need more time. It could be dangerous.'

But Mirabelle was already walking away.

Odd was starting to wish he hadn't come back.

Billy

Billy could see a chink of light along the edge of one of the planks of wood that had been hammered over the broken window as a temporary repair measure. He went and stood before it and ran his hands along the edges, feeling the warmth of wood and sunlight on his fingertips.

Back in London, he'd spent most of his time either in the grubby darkness of the cellar or on the night-shrouded streets. He would, of course, venture out during the day at the urging of the Catchpoles to get food because of his ability to blend in with humans. 'No sense in wasting your talent,' Ma Catchpole used to say to him.

It was quiet in the house now, and Billy listened hard to what might lie outside, but he detected nothing. He hooked his fingers under the edge of a plank then wrenched it free, flinging it into a corner with one swift movement.

He made short work of the rest of the planks and soon sunlight flooded the room. A warm breeze came through the opening.

Billy slung his satchel across his shoulder, hopped up on to the windowsill then leapt to the small roof below, which jutted out over the grounds. This time there was no panicked grasping and grappling in mid-air. He slid one-handed down a drainpipe, reaching the ground in no time.

The sky was blue and streaked with wisps of cloud. Billy walked away from the house, marvelling at the space that surrounded him. He was used to being hemmed in by buildings and people. To him this was a strange new paradise. He felt a pang when he remembered that Meg wasn't with him. She'd like it here, he thought. He wished she were here now, walking with him. He tensed, now thinking about what he had to do to ensure her safety. If he could just make sure not to draw any more attention to himself . . .

Two small birds flitted past, startling him for a moment. Billy watched them bob and dip together before they finally disappeared behind the roof.

Something else caught his eye. Something larger and darker. A raven sat hunched on the corner of a low stone wall only a few feet away from him. It had one good eye; the other was blurred and milky. It whirred its feathers for a moment, then cawed at him.

Billy tilted his head. The raven blinked its eye as it regarded him. Billy was sure it was studying him. He knelt down, took his satchel off and laid his book on the grass, then held his hand out.

The raven angled its head and blinked again.

Billy snapped his fingers. The raven took flight and landed directly on his hand. Billy stood up and smiled at it, marvelling at the dark inky-blue sheen of its feathers. As close as the raven was now, it seemed indifferent to him in that way only birds can be, twitching its head this way and that without once looking directly at him. Billy stroked its head and the raven didn't protest.

'His name is Lucius,' said a voice behind him.

Billy turned to find Mirabelle coming towards him. The raven flew from Billy's hand and landed on her shoulder. Mirabelle smiled and stroked his beak.

'He likes you,' said Mirabelle. 'He has a good sense for people, he knows you're a friend.'

Billy nodded at her, but his eyes flicked away for a moment when she used that word.

Friend.

If she only knew the truth . . .

'I saw you from the window,' said Mirabelle. 'Everyone else is usually asleep during daytime.' She looked at him tentatively, almost hopefully. 'Do you sleep?'

Billy shook his head.

'Neither do I. What about eating. Do you eat?'

Billy shook his head again. 'No.'

'Ever?'

Mirabelle was biting her lip now. Billy thought the way she was looking at him was strange.

'Never,' he said.

Mirabelle looked about ready to hop out of her skin with delight. 'Me neither.' She frowned. 'Well, that's not strictly true. There was one time . . .' She shook her head. 'You don't need to know.' Her attention was drawn to the ground. 'What's that?'

Billy had forgotten his book. He leaned down and picked it up.

Mirabelle stepped closer to him and held her hand out. 'Can I see?'

Billy felt a mild flutter of panic, but he steeled himself and held the book out for her. Mirabelle took it.

'*Treasure Island*,' she said. She looked at him and smiled. 'Is it good?'

'Yes,' said Billy. He was fighting the urge to snatch it back from her. Thorne's words were ringing in his ears.

You need to blend in, boy. Act normal.

He didn't think snatching his book from a stranger's hand would be considered 'acting normal' so he restrained himself, even as Mirabelle opened the cover and ran her hands over the title page.

'It has your name in it,' she said, holding the page open.

In faint pencil it said, *Billy, March 23rd, 1939*.

'That's not me,' said Billy. 'That's someone else.'

Mirabelle frowned.

'When I was . . .'

Billy didn't want to tell her. He didn't want to tell anyone. Why should he? But there was something about Mirabelle, something nice. She'd been by his side when that Mavis woman had been so awful towards him. She'd defended him when the other children had been teasing him back in his room.

The torrent of words surprised him.

'I was found, my . . . two people found me when I was very young. I was abandoned during the war, and this was left with me.' He shook his head. 'The Catchpoles gave me my name, and when I started to read I realised my name was in the book. It was like it found me . . .'

Billy's cheeks felt as if they were on fire. Mirabelle handed the book to him and he took it from her.

'Foundlings. Enoch told me about them. Sometimes children like us were abandoned.'

Billy considered the information. 'I've always felt a bit different, and the Catchpoles once used that same word...'

'Misbegotten,' said Mirabelle.

Billy nodded.

He felt a new feeling now. Something strange and, dare he think it, possibly wonderful. It was as if he and Mirabelle were somehow connected by an invisible tether. He'd only ever felt that way once before, and that was with Meg. It was an overwhelming sensation, almost dizzying. He smiled tentatively.

Mirabelle nodded at the book he was now clutching to his chest.

'Must be a good book,' she said, 'and it's obviously important to you.'

Billy nodded vigorously. All of a sudden, he felt like crying and he didn't know why. He wiped an eye. 'Yes, yes, it is.' The words just seemed to tumble out of him now. 'Thank you for looking out for me earlier, for sticking up for me. No one's ever . . .'

No one's ever done that for me, was what he was trying to say, but the words seemed to get stuck in his throat, as if saying them might release something that would crush him.

Mirabelle nodded sympathetically. 'We have a lot in common, Billy. We should be friends. After all, we're nearly more than family.'

She smiled at him, and now Billy felt sick and slightly ashamed. He was trembling slightly.

Blend in. Act normal. Pretend to be one of them. Make friends if you have to. Think of your sister.

'I wanted to invite you to something,' said Mirabelle.

'Really?' said Billy, hoping she wouldn't notice the fact that he was trembling. Lucius was still looking at him, almost inquisitively.

'I'm having a special event before the Configuration begins. A pre-celebration, if you like. I'm organising it for tonight. I thought you might be able to help me.'

Back at the house, Mirabelle showed him the invitations she'd made. They were handwritten in ink on small white cards. Billy marvelled at the lovely fluid grace of Mirabelle's writing. Each one read:

You are hereby cordially invited to a special celebration at midnight tonight in the Room of Lights. This will be a special and unique event to mark the build-up to the Great Configuration. Looking forward to seeing you there.

Kind regards,
Mirabelle of Rookhaven

They spent the rest of the morning running around the house, shoving the invitations under everyone's bedroom doors. Mirabelle made a game of it and decided they would compete to see who could get rid of their invitations as quickly as possible. Billy raced ahead, nimble and quick. He could vault six steps at a time, and he was at least twice as fast as Mirabelle. At one point he leapt from the top of a banister to the floor above, his satchel swinging as he jumped. He felt a low almost animal hum within himself, a sense of exhilaration that made him feel free. Halfway through his efforts, he felt a twinge of guilt and slowed down, dawdling for a bit.

He met Mirabelle waiting for him in the hallway. She beamed at him.

'Looks like I won.'

Billy smiled shyly.

His head suddenly snapped round when he heard something like a whisper. His eyes were drawn to the dark opening behind him. He couldn't see what lay beyond it, but he could have sworn the sound had emanated from there.

'What's down there?' he asked.

Mirabelle seemed almost pleased that he'd asked.

'You'll find out,' she said, smiling enigmatically. 'Come on, let's go back outside.'

Mirabelle took Billy to a small copse of trees. They sat there a while and talked to each other, all Billy's thoughts of reading his book forgotten. Mirabelle told him a story about a monster. A creature called the Malice, which had been vanquished five years ago on these very grounds. The description of the creature gave Billy chills. Mirabelle was animated, almost excited, by the story, but Billy noticed the abrupt change in tone when she spoke about her friend Jem and Jem's brother Tom. The brother and sister had stayed for just over a year in the house. Mirabelle had considered Jem to be her best friend, but one day she'd told Mirabelle that she and Tom were leaving.

'I suppose it was for the best,' said Mirabelle, plucking at some strands of grass.

Billy frowned. 'Why?'

Mirabelle seemed surprised by the question. 'Well, we're not like them. For humans, it's different. They age and grow, and they get on with their lives, and maybe living here wasn't for her. I think they needed to be with their own people.' Mirabelle shrugged. 'Jem and I wrote to each other for a while, but her letters have stopped. Enoch says that's what humans do. They forget. Lose touch.'

Mirabelle looked off into the middle distance, still twisting grass in her hand. On a branch above her, Lucius stood sentinel.

'I see,' said Billy, feeling the need to say something, even though he didn't fully understand. 'Did you know your parents?' he asked.

Mirabelle smiled. 'I met my mother once.' She shook her head. 'Although it's hard to explain how.'

'What about your father?'

A curious look came into Mirabelle's eyes that Billy couldn't read.

'No,' she said. 'I've never really thought about him. No one knows who he was. It's like he never even existed.'

'You didn't ask your mother?'

'I couldn't.'

Billy frowned.

'Like I said, it's hard to explain, but I have family here, and that's enough,' said Mirabelle.

'I don't remember my parents,' said Billy.

'I'm sorry to hear that.'

Meg is my family, Billy wanted to say, but he stopped himself.

Mirabelle stood up. 'I stopped you reading your book. I'll let you get back to it. Thanks for listening, Billy.'

Billy shook his head to imply that it was nothing. He watched Mirabelle walk back to the house. She turned round for an instant.

'Don't forget midnight,' she shouted.

Billy nodded.

He caught sight of Lucius watching him from the branch above. Lucius cawed at him then took flight and followed after Mirabelle.

Piglet

Midnight.

Piglet is giddy with excitement. He's not really sure why, but it feels as if every part of him is beating in time with his heart and, when the door opens, he has to resist the urge to launch himself out into the hallway.

He must remember to do as he is told.

'Do as you're told.'

These are the words that Mirabelle uses. The words she always uses. Odd is with her. Odd doesn't use any words at all. Piglet knows that he can't because Odd is too frightened. Piglet can smell his fear.

Mirabelle says something about Odd to Piglet, and Piglet tries really hard to listen, he really does. But Odd looks so funny standing there, so pale, so nervous, so small. Piglet wonders what has him so frightened.

Mirabelle has asked Piglet a question. Piglet thinks hard about what she has asked, then nods to show he understands.

Mirabelle looks at Odd. She speaks more words. To Piglet they are like leaves tossed about in a breeze, but he manages to hear them.

'Then it's time,' *she says.*

Piglet takes a deep breath.

He is ready.

Billy

Billy waited until the last moment to head to the Room of Lights. He'd already tortured himself with the best way to go about it. He'd considered arriving early, but that might have meant being accosted by people like Mavis or others who might corner him and question him about his right to be there. He thought maybe arriving late might do the trick, but then there was the problem of drawing attention to himself as the last person in.

There was only one thing for it. He had to arrive a moment or two before Mirabelle in the hope that whatever she had planned would be enough of a distraction. There was no way out of it. He'd promised her that he would be present. The happy almost pleading way her eyes had shone as she'd begged him to come along had made him feel more guilty than ever. She was going out of her way to welcome him, but only he knew the real reason he was here, and he felt bad about his deception.

As dozens of people filed into the Room of Lights, Billy hunched his shoulders and lowered his eyes to the floor in an attempt to make himself as inconspicuous as possible. The babble around him was filled with querulous and confused voices. One man slapped his hand against one of Mirabelle's invitations.

'I mean really. How utterly vulgar. It's like a cheap circus flyer.'

The man's bulky rhino-faced companion, dressed in a luxuriant fur coat, grunted in what Billy took to be a sign of agreement.

As they entered the room, the people started to mingle and converse. There was almost constant movement and chatter, which suited Billy down to the ground because no one seemed to be paying attention to him. Except . . .

He felt a prickling along his spine and in a break in the crowd he spotted the hooded figure of Winthropp just standing there, hands clasped behind his back, looking straight at him.

Billy ducked under the impossibly long legs of someone called Uncle Jeremy, who was bending down to talk to a bird-faced woman. He headed for a corner in an attempt to avoid the attentions of Winthropp.

'Young Master Catchpole.'

A hand clasped his shoulder. Billy wheeled round, ready to let fly with his fists should the moment merit it.

He found himself looking up into the dark eyes of Enoch.

'I didn't consider you to be one who was partial to social occasions,' said Enoch.

Billy didn't know what to say. He was about to turn away from Enoch when something else took hold of him.

It felt as if his whole body had been electrified. His hair stood on end. The skin on his forearms tingled. He felt the almost unbearable urge to run, right now, to get out of here, to go anywhere.

Enoch frowned and Billy knew he felt it too. Not as strongly maybe, but he knew.

There was something approaching. Something wild. Powerful.

Dangerous.

Billy bolted. He pushed people aside, ignoring their complaints. He caught sight of Winthropp again, just for a second, those silver eyes burning into him.

Billy was only a few feet from the door when Mirabelle entered the room. He stopped dead.

Mirabelle looked at the expectant crowd. She smiled at them.

'Welcome, everyone. I'm so glad you could all make it for this very special occasion.'

There were murmurs now, the sound of which angered Billy. They were filled with haughtiness and complacency. *Didn't they know? Couldn't they feel it? Something terrible was making its approach.*

To Billy it felt as if a vast thundercloud were heaving its weight high up above them all, ready to unleash hell. He wanted to run, but Mirabelle was blocking the only exit. He waved frantically to try to get her attention, but she seemed oblivious to him as she smiled at the crowd.

She clasped her hands together. 'Ladies and gentlemen, if you would be so kind. We have a very special guest tonight.'

Odd stepped through the door. To Billy he looked paler than ever, and there was something else in the way that he walked, his shoulders tight, his steps a little too stilted. There was someone else with him.

Odd gestured for his companion to step into the room.

The boy was maybe a foot shorter than Odd. He had dark hair and a pale round face, and in those respects he looked quite ordinary, but Billy could see his eyes. For a moment they were the enquiring eyes of a child, looking, seeking, as if seeing the world for the first time. Then they changed colour from grey, to blue, to black. Billy was shaking now, his head pounding.

Mirabelle stepped aside for the boy and announced to the room: 'For the first time, indeed on the occasion of his very first social engagement . . .'

The whole room held its breath. Billy felt as if his skull were about to explode.

Mirabelle smiled.

'. . . May I present Piglet,' she said.

There was a brief stunned silence.

Then the screaming started.

Mirabelle

In hindsight, Mirabelle realised she shouldn't have been surprised at the reaction. Truth be told, she hadn't really thought *what* the reaction might be. She'd just presumed that everyone would have been just as delighted as she was that she'd taught Piglet how to mingle safely among members of the Family. She hadn't reckoned with his age-old reputation as being somehow 'dangerous'. She'd hoped that his help in breaking the influence of the Malice might have redeemed his name in some way. Unfortunately, it seemed that Family members were still terrified of the idea of a powerful entity with the ability to invade their minds at will, even if that entity did look like a child.

'Are you sure about this?' Odd had asked when she'd told him her plan all those months ago. Mirabelle was adamant that it could work.

'I'm absolutely certain,' she said.

'I'm not,' sighed Odd.

Odd told her that they should inform Enoch of her plan. Mirabelle had objected straight away. She wouldn't hear of it. She'd taken great delight in the look of horror on Odd's face when she'd told him she'd already started making inroads into teaching Piglet how to behave in human form. At first there were the daily visits to Piglet's room 'just to talk'. Then there were the times when she'd actually leave the door open behind her. At this revelation Odd's face had turned a remarkable shade of grey. She asked if he could help her, just to be there as an extra calming presence.

'You mean someone else to share the blame,' Odd had said.

He'd eventually and reluctantly agreed to help. Mirabelle suspected he did this only because he was hoping to dissuade her at some point, but she'd already decided that she wasn't going to be swayed. It was Mirabelle's opinion that Piglet deserved to be among his family, not cooped up alone in the depths of the house. All it would take was some gentle cajoling, both with Piglet and the rest of her family. She was certain of it.

Talking to Piglet took up a lot of time. He wasn't the most attentive student, and his mind tended to wander, at least that's what Mirabelle presumed the constant shape-shifting signified. Eventually he started to calm down, and sometimes he might even pass half an hour fixed in the same shape. One day he listened while transformed into a giant black dog with two heads. On another day he was similarly attentive while taking on the form of a pulsating gold vapour. Mirabelle knew she was finally getting through to him when he stayed fixed.

Then it was on to the next stage. 'Presenting himself in a suitably acceptable fashion for the delectation of ordinary members of society,' as Odd put it.

They needed Piglet to take on the shape of someone

or something inoffensive enough to not frighten people. It took some time, but eventually he seemed happy to settle on the form of a small boy, a boy who seemed quiet and alert, and who didn't speak. This seemed to be the one hurdle they couldn't get over. Piglet didn't seem to want to use words. As Odd pointed out, a creature who preferred to communicate with people via their very minds probably found words a little too slow and clumsy. Mirabelle supposed it made sense.

And now here they were, standing in the Room of Lights, confronted by a rippling sea of panicked Family members, quite a few of them shrieking in blind terror.

Most of them recoiled as if trying to melt into the very walls. Mirabelle heard Aunt Mavis wailing: 'No! No! We must flee! We must flee!'

Mirabelle raised her hands in an effort to call for calm.

'It's all right. He's been told to behave. We've been training him for months.'

'Well, you instigated it, Mirabelle,' Odd announced to all present. 'To be fair, I joined the project at quite a late stage.'

Mirabelle glowered at him, then turned her attention back to the crowd.

'I assure you, there's nothing to be afraid of. I've made him promise to stay in this form and not to go poking around in anyone's mind.'

A few people frowned. Some of them even cocked their heads in curiosity. Mirabelle sensed a subtle shift in the room. If she could just convince them . . .

Then Piglet took a step forward.

There was even more screaming now, and Mirabelle spotted Uncle Reginald scuttling up the walls in beetle form, while the few Family members who could fly took to the air. Aunt Mavis was frantically waving her lace handkerchief in front of her face, while her sons held her arms as if fearing she might faint. And yet in the midst of all the commotion two figures stood out.

One was Billy, who seemed utterly transfixed by the sight of Piglet. Mirabelle had never seen anyone so tense. It was as if all his muscles were quivering. His eyes were huge and dark. Meanwhile, another figure lurked on the periphery of the chaos. Winthropp stood with his hands behind his back, quietly observing everything.

The noise and activity came to a sudden halt when a figure took to the air and landed between Mirabelle and the crowd and shouted:

'ENOUGH!'

Enoch's eyes blazed as he looked out over the assembled Family members, almost daring one of them to step out of line. The silence was only broken by some soft gibbering from Aunt Mavis.

Enoch turned his attention to Mirabelle.

'Explain yourself.'

Mirabelle bristled slightly at his tone. 'Do I have to? Really, Uncle, I think it's quite obvious—'

'Mirabelle!'

Mirabelle sighed and looked at the ceiling.

'I just thought it would be nice.'

'Nice?'

'Yes. I thought with the Configuration happening it would be a good time to introduce Piglet to the rest of his family. I think he should be allowed some freedom.'

'And you didn't think to ask permission first?'

'This is Mirabelle we're talking about,' Odd muttered.

Mirabelle shot him a look while he pretended to examine his cuffs. Murmurs and whispers began to drift around the room, a pocket of panic here, a core of indignation there. The murmurs began to build to a general hubbub, while Enoch looked at Piglet and frowned.

The murmuring turned to screams again when Piglet took another step forward. Mavis swooned and the Dibble twins failed to catch her. Uncle Urg shrieked in panic, demanding that Siegfried deposit him inside his jacket for safe keeping.

Enoch turned and glared at the audience again, raising his hand for silence.

Piglet looked calm and slightly detached, as if he couldn't understand the impact he was having on everyone.

Enoch stepped forward. There were gasps as he went down on one knee in front of Piglet and started to examine his face. Even Mirabelle was surprised. She could see Billy out of the corner of her eye, still quivering.

'How long can he maintain this form?' asked Enoch.

'As long as he wants,' Mirabelle said. 'As long as

he's told to,' she added hurriedly.

'Really?' said Enoch, his tone surprisingly relaxed.

'Yes, I've been training him for months.'

'Without my permission,' said Enoch, still studying Piglet's face.

Mirabelle lowered her head slightly. 'Yes.'

'I take it you've told him he's not permitted to touch anybody?'

'Of course,' said Mirabelle.

'Good,' said Enoch.

He stood up and walked round Piglet. Piglet followed him with his eyes, and then the most curious thing happened, and Mirabelle felt her heart skip a beat.

Piglet smiled.

When Enoch smiled in response, Odd whispered, 'I don't believe it.' Mirabelle felt lightheaded with glee.

Enoch bowed to Piglet. 'Welcome, Piglet.'

Piglet bowed in response.

The room was filled with 'oohs' and 'ahs' of wonder now, but Mirabelle couldn't help notice that Billy was still tensed.

Enoch politely but firmly asked everyone but Odd, Mirabelle and Piglet to leave the room. Mirabelle guided Piglet to a corner to allow everyone else to leave through the door unimpeded. She noticed the quick furtive glances most of them gave him, saw them muttering among themselves and she heard the word 'dangerous' used more than once. She looked unflinchingly at every person that looked in their direction.

Finally, with the door closed, and with no one else present, Enoch turned his attention to her.

'Can you control him?'

'It's not about *control*,' said Mirabelle. 'He's not a pet.'

'I think we all know that, Mirabelle. I'm asking you whether you can promise me that Piglet will do no harm.'

Mirabelle looked at Piglet, who now seemed preoccupied with the lights hanging in the air.

'I promise,' she said.

Enoch seemed to consider her response. She realised now might be the best time to act and tell him about the rest of her plan. She didn't want to lose any slim advantage she might have, and she decided now was not the time to dither.

'There's one other thing, Uncle. Something I need to do. I made a promise.'

Piglet

Piglet looks at the lights. There are so many different colours, so much beauty, and when he looks at them he seems to remember something . . .

Then the memory is gone, snatched, drifting, vanished, like something carried away on a breeze, but Piglet has felt the edges of it, and it is warm and comforting.

Someone is saying something.

Piglet turns to see Enoch with his hands on his hips looking down at Mirabelle. She has her hands on her hips also. They speak to each other with their funny little words, and they say them louder to each other with each passing moment. Eventually, Enoch rolls his eyes and sighs and Mirabelle folds her arms and looks . . .

Happy – that's it.

Piglet is slightly distracted now by a more recent memory.

He thinks about the boy staring at him when he first walked into the room. There was a scent from him, a mixture of anger and fear, and a dark wildness in his eyes. Piglet wonders why he is this way. Ordinarily, he would investigate why, but he has been told by Mirabelle to behave, and he has to control his curiosity.

But Piglet likes to know things, and surely it wouldn't hurt just to look.

Yet he knows
this would only
disappoint
Mirabelle, and
he doesn't want
to disappoint her.

When Odd
and Mirabelle walk
him back to his room,
Mirabelle seems really happy.
She chatters quite a bit, while Odd stays quiet.

Before he steps back into his room Piglet looks at his hands. This body is small and slow, but Mirabelle seems to be delighted with his new form. Piglet supposes it will suffice for now. He finds it hard to resist the urge to change, but he knows it is important to Mirabelle and he wants to please her, because she has always been kind to him.

Before she closes the door, Mirabelle says one more word to him.

'Tomorrow.'

She smiles.

The door closes.

Tomorrow.

The word means nothing to Piglet. He expands, he dissipates, he fills the darkness in his room.

But even though the word means nothing to him, Piglet knows time is passing. Night ticks by. The moon pales as the sky brightens. He feels the rising of the sun and its movement across *the sky. He also senses it sinking as evening approaches. All this happens so much faster for him than for the likes of Mirabelle. He feels every moment as it passes, and he knows there will come a point soon when something will happen. He is not sure what yet, but he senses it. A change of sorts. Something that will ripple outwards and transform everything it touches. It will not be Mirabelle's 'tomorrow'. It will be something else she doesn't even suspect.*

It will be something new.

And for some reason he thinks again about the boy, and those wild, dark eyes.

Odd

Odd was surprised by how well everything had gone the previous night. He could almost have admitted to feeling a sense of contentment, although when he really thought about it that might have been pushing it. He still felt a little uneasy about Mirabelle's new project. He didn't share her confidence, and he certainly didn't share it when it came to the next stage, a stage to which he believed Enoch had agreed a little too readily.

But now he found himself waiting in the hallway as evening fell. He was the designated 'escort', as Enoch called him. Odd protested weakly, pointing out to Enoch what exactly he might be able to do if there was what he called a 'crisis'. Enoch ignored his protests.

Then there was the thing that perturbed him most of all, the use of his gift in this particular instance. Odd had finally got used to having other people accompany him through his portals in recent years, but this new development was something entirely more troubling for him.

Mirabelle stepped from the corridor leading down towards Piglet's room. Piglet followed a couple of feet behind her. He was in the guise of the same inoffensive-looking little boy, but that didn't provide Odd with any comfort.

'Ready?' asked Mirabelle. Her eyes were sparkling and Odd had never seen her look so excited. Despite his fear of Piglet, he actually felt moved by Mirabelle's enthusiasm. He supposed it was good for her, especially as it provided a welcome distraction from her preoccupation with the fact that she hadn't heard from Jem in months.

'Yes,' said Odd. He could sense the others stirring in the house. It was probably best they left now before somebody saw them and there was another scene. He couldn't deal with another bout of hysteria from the likes of Aunt Mavis.

He twirled a finger in the air and an inky black portal opened up before him. He could already smell the fresh air wafting from their destination. He gestured for Mirabelle and Piglet to step through with him. There was a rushing sensation and a quiet pop. Odd blinked, taking in their surroundings.

They were standing on the road leading into the village just as Mirabelle had requested. She'd suggested that a stroll might do Piglet some good.

They headed towards the village. Mirabelle had to keep reminding Piglet to keep up with them as he became distracted by things like blades of grass at the roadside, or a leaf hanging from a branch.

'I think he's doing very well,' she said to Odd, perhaps a little defensively.

'I think so too,' said Odd.

Mirabelle looked at him suspiciously. 'Really?'

'Yes,' said Odd, trying his best to convince not just her but also himself.

Mirabelle stared at him. Odd began to feel a slight prickle of discomfort.

'Odd? What is it?'

'Well, I mean, it's very laudable to be teaching Piglet how to behave outside his room . . .'

'But?'

Odd stopped in his tracks. '*Why* are you doing it?'

Mirabelle looked at him. Behind them, Piglet had picked up a pebble and was examining it closely between thumb and forefinger.

'What do you mean?' said Mirabelle. 'Isn't it obvious? I'm doing it because I want Piglet to be part of the Family. He should be allowed to roam free inside the house.'

'But he *is* part of the Family. He's always been part of the Family.'

'What? You mean locked away down there in that dungeon of his?'

Odd made a face. 'It's hardly a dungeon now, is it?'

'It might as well be.'

Mirabelle cocked her nose in the air and started to walk away from him.

'Mirabelle.'

Odd trotted after her. She was swinging her arms furiously by her sides. 'Come along, Piglet,' she called.

Odd caught up, trying to keep pace with her.

'I understand, Mirabelle, really I do. I just wonder if

you've taken on a little too much . . .'

For the wrong reasons, was what he wanted to say, but he couldn't bring himself to utter the words. He'd known Mirabelle long enough to know that sometimes she needed to distract herself, and her project with Piglet seemed to be the perfect excuse for her to immerse herself in something that might stop her thinking about Jem. Mirabelle liked to keep herself busy. Odd liked to go to new places. He knew all about distractions. He supposed he could bring up the subject of Jem, but he was reluctant because he knew it would only hurt Mirabelle to talk about it.

'Look at him, Odd. Does he look like he's a little *too much to take on?*'

Piglet was now examining a twig. He turned it over and over in his hands before finally sticking it in his mouth and nibbling on it.

'You're still afraid of him, aren't you?' said Mirabelle.

Odd sighed. 'Yes, I suppose I am a little. He's still like a child in many ways. A child who can turn into a six-headed dragon on a whim. A child who can't seem to control his impulse to go poking around in the nooks and crannies of people's minds. It's a very disconcerting gift.'

'You shouldn't be afraid of him. He's family.'

Odd looked at Piglet standing there, nibbling contentedly on his twig.

'Right now, he reminds me of poor old Bertram,' he said. 'I miss Bertram.' Uncle Bertram had been bumbling and distracted in almost everything he did, but he had been loving, and fierce when he needed to be, protecting the Family with his life, which he had sacrificed unthinkingly against the Malice. Despite his years, Bertram had also had a childlike sense of wonder. In that sense, he was perhaps not unlike Piglet.

'So do I,' said Mirabelle, smiling sadly.

'I'm sorry, Mirabelle. I'm just a worrier.'

Mirabelle punched him playfully on the arm. 'There's nothing to worry about.'

'I'll take your word for it.'

They continued on their walk into the village. It was a calm night, the air was warm and Piglet would occasionally stop to look at the stars in the sky and have to be coaxed onwards by Mirabelle. The mood lightened between her and Odd, and the tension he'd been feeling started to fade. Maybe Mirabelle was right. Piglet was family, after all, and he seemed to have taken her instructions on-board and was behaving himself. Odd felt a glimmer of optimism. There and then he made a decision. He thought he would surprise Mirabelle when he reached their destination. He would prove to himself that he was not a coward. He would do the one thing that he'd been afraid of these past few months and then everything would move on and they'd all be happy. He would pop in and say hello to Marcus. In fact, now that he thought about it, he realised that a visit would lift both their spirits. Odd had heard humans talk about the recuperative qualities of sociable interaction. Maybe, just maybe, it might even do Marcus some good.

Odd felt his confidence and excitement growing with each step.

He was so pleased with his decision that he was actually smiling by the time they reached the house.

Mirabelle knocked, but as the door opened Odd's smile disappeared.

He saw Paul's eyes, the downturned mouth, the sorrowful shake of the head, and instantly he knew.

Mirabelle pushed Paul aside and ran into the house.

Piglet

Piglet looks at Odd. For some reason, he has fallen on to his knees, and his face is in his hands. The young man who opened the door is leaning against it as if his own legs won't support his weight. He is saying something to Odd over and over, but Odd doesn't seem to hear the words.

Piglet can hear Mirabelle inside the house.

He follows her in.

He feels strange, as if he is being drawn by an unseen power that compels him forward, and yet he also feels the urge to resist it.

It is very confusing.

Dr Ellenby is sitting slumped in a chair. His eyes are closed and Mirabelle's head is in her hands and she is sobbing.

Piglet stands beside her. He feels strange as he looks at Dr Ellenby. Hollow and alone, even though Mirabelle is with him.

After a while he puts a hand on her head.

He doesn't know why.

Part 3
The Configuration

Mirabelle

Mirabelle sat in a corner of the sitting room in Dr Ellenby's house while those around her engaged in muted conversation. She stared into space, her eyes burning, not seeing, not caring. Meanwhile, Lucius perched on the mantlepiece above her, glowering at all and sundry.

The funeral had been awful. Paul had sobbed his way through Reverend Dankworth's final oration at the graveside and Mirabelle had hated him for it.

And she had stood there like stone, as dirty grey clouds scudded overhead, and the wind wrapped itself round each mourner.

She only vaguely remembered getting to Dr Ellenby's in someone's car. She, Enoch and Eliza had come as representatives of the Family. It was a measure of how much he'd meant to them that they'd attended even in daylight. She'd seen Odd trail into the house sometime after the burial. He'd nodded at her briefly, but that was the extent of his interaction with her. Meanwhile, there was a constant stream of mourners coming into the house. Mirabelle tried to block them out, their shuffling, their muttering. It was all becoming too suffocating.

Then someone touched her hand and knelt down before her, and when she saw those familiar blue eyes she thought the thing that seemed to be tightening in her chest might finally snap.

'Mirabelle.'

'Freddie!' Mirabelle gasped.

Freddie squeezed her hand; he was looking more like his older brother James every day. There was a confidence in the way he carried himself that was so unlike the village boy she'd watched grow up.

'Are you all right?' Freddie asked.

Mirabelle could only shake her head.

Freddie winced. 'Stupid question, sorry.'

Elizabeth, his mother, approached and smiled at Mirabelle. Mirabelle felt a rushing dizzying feeling, part joy, part grief. Freddie's mother tried to smile, to speak, but in the end she could only hold her hand out. Mirabelle reached for it and they laced their fingers together and the world swam before Mirabelle's eyes.

'Well, he was a good man,' said Freddie's mother, her head turned sideways as if she couldn't bring herself to look at Mirabelle.

'Yes,' said Freddie. 'The best.'

'Remember when you thought your leg was broken after you fell off your bike?'

Freddie gave a rueful smile. 'Yes, Mum.'

'Howling you were. Loud enough to be heard in the next village. He had you walking in seconds. Amazing what recuperative powers lollipops have. I've never seen someone with a "broken leg" run across a room so fast.'

Freddie chuckled, and there was a moment of silence between them as they thought about their friend. Mr Fletcher came and joined them. He nodded at Mirabelle, his giant hands looking clumsy and awkward as they clasped a glass. Mirabelle gave him a weak smile in response.

'I hear it's the Configuration tonight,' said Mr Fletcher, in an attempt to make conversation.

'Yes,' said Mirabelle.

'Very important, so I'm told. Very important, Enoch says.'

Mirabelle said nothing. She couldn't think of anything less important at this moment in time.

She stood up.

'Excuse me, please. I need to do something.'

The Fletchers parted for her, and Mirabelle slipped through the crowds in the sitting room and hallway, went into the study and closed the door behind her.

The study was empty. For one terrible moment, she was gripped by a shuddering grief as she looked at Dr Ellenby's desk. She steeled herself and somehow managed to quell it. She started to rummage in the drawers. It didn't take her long to find what she was looking for. She clasped the pipe to her chest 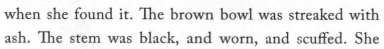 when she found it. The brown bowl was streaked with ash. The stem was black, and worn, and scuffed. She found the smell of old tobacco comforting.

'Bit quieter in here, isn't it?'

Mirabelle turned to find Odd standing just inside the door.

'Yes,' she said, averting her eyes.

'Enoch's been cornered by Mr Teasdale. He seems to be holding up quite well, despite the infliction of cat stories. I'm beginning to think that—'

'Why didn't you come to see him?'

Mirabelle was just as surprised by the tone of accusation in her voice as Odd seemed to be. He looked momentarily panicked, helpless.

'I mean you could have done it any time you wanted to. You are Odd, after all. Odd who can go anywhere, who can do what he likes. Odd, the very dear friend of Marcus Ellenby. Why? Why didn't you? You didn't even come to the burial, Odd!'

Odd shook his head. 'I . . . I don't know . . .'

Mirabelle stormed out. Her lasting image was of Odd looking pathetic and small as he feebly tried to gesture for her to stay.

In the hallway she looked from the front door down to the sitting room, her vision clouding again. She made her decision and snapped her fingers.

Lucius responded instantly and flew out of the sitting room, causing some people in the hallway to duck. As she turned to the door, Mirabelle was vaguely aware of Enoch frowning at her. He

132

might even have called out her name, but she didn't care.

Mirabelle left the house.

She wandered the village aimlessly at first, not sure where exactly she was going. She held the pipe so tightly she feared she might break it, but she seemed unable to unclench her hand. After stumbling around the laneways in the late evening light, she headed out on to the open road, with no thought of a destination, her mind dark and awhirl with thoughts of loss and pain.

Lucius took flight, and after a while some of his brethren joined him. The ravens flew in the gathering gloom above her, black, flapping, like Mirabelle's tormented thoughts made flesh.

She walked on into the night, her anger and sadness reaching upwards, sending tremors through the ravens.

Billy

'They put them in the ground and worms eat them.'

Billy was lurking behind a hedge, listening to Daisy breathlessly inform Dotty about human funeral customs. Enoch and some of the others had returned from the funeral hours ago, but there had been no sign of Mirabelle. Billy had spotted Odd looking forlornly down the length of the Path of Flowers at one point. He presumed he was waiting for Mirabelle. Eventually Odd gave up and went into the house.

'And in a wooden box?' gasped Dotty.

'Yes,' Daisy hissed, her eyes glowing with a sadistic delight.

'What's that, young lady?' asked Aunt Mavis, beckoning the twins to join her and a group of others who'd wandered out of the house. She was flanked by her sons. For some reason, a lot of the Family members had chosen to gather in the night air and chat together. There were at least a dozen of them. The whole house seemed to have been crackling with excitement and tension even during daylight hours today. Billy had come into the garden in search of solitude, but it seemed wherever he went he couldn't avoid anyone. The talk among the guests was all about the Configuration, and even he was getting a little tired of hearing about it.

Daisy and Dotty approached Aunt Mavis's group. Billy didn't like the tone of relish in Daisy's voice as she recounted what she'd been discussing with her sister.

'I was just talking about what the humans do to their dead,' she said.

'Their *dead?*' replied a high, querulous voice which Billy recognised as that of Uncle Urg.

'Surely you know what dead is, Urg?' growled someone from the back of the crowd.

'Dead is what happens to them when they cease to exist,' said Byron haughtily.

'Cease to exist?' A woman snorted. 'The very thought of it.'

'Quite a few of our number ceased to exist when the Malice found them,' said the rhino-faced man tightly.

The idea of this seemed to perturb most of those present, and there was awkward shuffling and shifty glances, along with some anxious grumbling.

'They put them in the ground and worms eat them, Aunt,' said Daisy proudly.

Mavis looked horrified. 'How utterly vulgar.'

Everyone started to babble now as they discussed the burial traditions of humans. Billy was intrigued for a moment, until he heard a voice behind him:

'What are *you* doing here?'

He wheeled round to find Winthropp standing there with his hands clasped behind his back.

'What?' said Billy.

'I said, what are you doing here?'

Winthropp's voice was strange, hollow and rasping, like skittering leaves on stone. It was dry and horrid, and sounded as if it came from somewhere else and not from the face contained within that hood.

'I was going for a walk,' said Billy.

Winthropp shook his head slowly. Billy couldn't tell whether it was with pity or contempt, although he had a suspicion it was a bit of both. Those silver eyes were piercing. Billy found he couldn't tear his own gaze away from them.

'That's not what I meant. That's not what I meant at all,' said Winthropp.

Billy's hackles were raised now – he felt cornered. He was just about to snarl something in response when he heard and smelt something familiar, and his attention was drawn away from his interrogator.

Mirabelle had just made her way through the gate with Lucius on her shoulder, and was now standing before the babbling crowd. One by one they fell silent.

Mavis pushed herself to the front of the crowd.

'Your uncle was looking for you, young lady. You're late, and on the very evening of the Configuration. Explain yourself.'

Mirabelle looked exhausted.

'I don't have to explain myself to anyone,' she said wearily.

It was night, but even so Billy noticed that some ravens

were now nestling in the branches of nearby trees. A few more were wheeling around in the sky. He sniffed the air. It smelt odd, tangy almost, as if electrified. His skin prickled.

Mavis put her hands on her hips and wiggled with contempt. 'I suppose you were busy with that nonsense in the village.'

Mirabelle raised her head. Billy could see the glint of anger in her eyes. Lucius snapped his wings, some of his brethren in the trees following suit.

'Nonsense?' said Mirabelle coldly.

Mavis jabbed the air with a finger. 'Yes, indeed. Nonsense. The very idea of their rituals. It's uncouth. Why you even bothered to go there I cannot fathom.'

Both Byron and Vernon nodded in agreement. Some of the crowd muttered among themselves.

Mirabelle clenched her fists. Her whole body was quivering. 'He was my friend.'

'*Was*, yes. What a strange thing, being gone like that. *Dying*, I think they call it. To be honest, I regard it as little more than a moral failing. Absolutely pathetic, if you ask me. One of your sisters was regaling us here with details about what happens afterwards. Apparently, they put their kind in the ground and they're eaten by worms!'

Mirabelle raised her fists.

Billy had never seen so many ravens move together so fast. They took flight as one. At first, they were just a scattering, then they coalesced with frightening speed into a dense, inky-black cloud. They engulfed Mavis within seconds, and all that could be heard was her high-pitched shrieking through a flapping tumult of wings. Her sons tried to wade into the tempest, but were beaten back by the sheer force of numbers. The rest of the Family members drew back towards the house, some of them squealing in terror. The Dibble twins were reduced to crawling on the ground in an effort to reach their mother. They were gibbering and crying. One of them went reeling backwards as a raven took him full in the face. Mirabelle stood watching it all, standing ramrod straight with her fists raised, her eyes blazing. Despite the savagery of it all, Billy couldn't help but marvel at her.

Mirabelle lowered her arms, loosened her fingers and the ravens departed. An eerie silence descended as they took flight and dispersed into the night sky. Lucius gave a low throaty caw from Mirabelle's shoulder as if in approval.

A bedraggled Mavis tried to pull herself up into a standing position while her whimpering sons attempted to help her. Some of the crowd inched back, curious despite their fear. Mirabelle looked at them defiantly, as if daring them to say anything.

Billy heard something else flapping, something larger, heavier. He watched as Enoch descended from the sky and, without breaking stride, advanced towards Mirabelle.

'What is the meaning of this?' he shouted.

Mavis raised a quivering hand. 'She . . . she set those wretched things on me!'

Enoch looked from Mirabelle to Mavis and back again.

'Is this true, Mirabelle?'

Mirabelle flapped a hand at him, almost in disgust. The gesture seemed to enrage him. He pointed at the house.

'Inside! Now!'

Mirabelle sighed and trudged towards the house. The crowd of fearful onlookers parted for her. The Dibble twins had helped their whimpering mother into a sitting position. Eventually, Enoch followed Mirabelle, as did the rest of the Family members. It was only then that Billy remembered his questioner.

He turned to look at Winthropp.

But Winthropp was gone.

Billy felt relief wash over him. He didn't like the strange silver-eyed imp. His gaze felt as if it could crush you.

The garden was silent now, but Billy could still feel that peculiar crackle of energy in the air that seemed to emanate from the house. He wondered how Meg was. He could see her face now. So help him, if those men hurt her . . .

His whole body tensed. Now was the time to act – to do what he'd been sent here for. He reached into his satchel and closed his hand around the orb.

Odd

Odd had watched the incident from an upstairs window. It was only a few hours until midnight and the Configuration. Everybody was already skittish, excited, perhaps even frightened about what was to come, and then the explosive incident involving Mirabelle had added even more tension to an already heightened mix of emotions. Even Odd had been horrified by the ravens' attack on Mavis. He'd watched it as if observing a dream. It just didn't seem real.

He headed downstairs as soon as he saw Enoch and Mirabelle coming back towards the house. He stood on the top stair, looking down, as Mirabelle burst through the front door, followed by Enoch.

Odd knew what to expect next.

'Young lady!'

Mirabelle wheeled round as Enoch shouted at her.

'I'm hardly *young*, Uncle,' Mirabelle jeered.

Some of the people from the garden had followed and were now creeping in around the door to have a look, while also making sure to keep a safe distance. More people were spilling out of various doorways and tentatively entering the hall to watch. Eliza was one of them, and she looked up questioningly at Odd. Odd could only shake his head in response.

A dishevelled Mavis was being carried in through the front door by her sons.

'You will apologise to your aunt NOW,' said Enoch.

Mirabelle's eyes flicked from Mavis to Enoch and back again. She sniffed.

'No. I won't.'

Odd held his breath, along with everybody else.

Enoch advanced towards Mirabelle. His voice was low, but it still carried around the hallway.

'No one who is of the Family may harm another member of the Family.'

Mirabelle looked up at him. 'True, but you forget, Uncle. I'm not strictly Family. I'm Misbegotten, as Aunt Mavis has kindly already said.'

Whispers flittered among the crowd. For a moment, Enoch looked unsure of himself. The air crackled with tension. From far away, Odd could hear the beginnings of a long, low moan from Piglet's room. The moan began to build and build . . .

'You are forbidden to attend the Configuration tonight,' said Enoch.

Mirabelle blinked and almost rocked back on her heels. From the depths of the house, Piglet howled.

'What?' Mirabelle said.

'You heard me. As punishment for attacking a member of the Family, you are hereby sanctioned. You will not be permitted to take part in the Configuration.'

Mirabelle shook her head in disbelief. Eliza took half

a step forward as if to protest.

Mirabelle looked around wildly. 'But I have to be allowed. I've never seen it.'

'Well, you'll have to wait another hundred years, then,' said Enoch.

Odd felt some sympathy for Mirabelle. She seemed to be struggling to take this in. Out of the corner of his eye he could see Eliza looking pleadingly at Enoch, while Enoch studiously ignored her.

'This will be my final word on the matter,' he thundered to all assembled.

He stormed off as the remaining Family members looked around awkwardly, slightly shamefaced. One by one, they started to disperse, leaving a bereft Mirabelle in the hallway.

Eliza moved towards her. 'Mirabelle—'

But Mirabelle ignored her and headed in the direction of Piglet's room with Lucius on her shoulder.

Odd sat down on the step, feeling suddenly weary. Eliza made her way up to him. He attempted a faltering smile.

'Well, it's been an eventful day all round,' he said.

'Indeed,' said Eliza.

Odd nodded. To put words on it seemed to require too much effort, as if he were afraid that speaking them might add more weight to the strange burden he now felt.

'She was wrong to do what she did,' said Eliza.

Odd shrugged.

'And yet Mavis deserved it, I suppose,' she said.

'I wouldn't dream of offering a defence, Aunt. It would be unseemly of me. Besides, Enoch would be offended.'

'I'll speak to Enoch,' said Eliza. 'I'll see if I can get him to change his mind.'

'He won't listen.'

'And what will you do?'

Odd looked at her curiously. There seemed to be a challenge of some sort in the way she eyed him. He shifted on the step, flapping the hem of his jacket behind him.

'What do you mean?'

'Where will you go?'

'Go?'

She appraised him coolly. Odd tried his best to keep looking her in the eye.

'I won't be going anywhere.'

'You always go somewhere.'

Odd pulled at his collar.

Eliza bent down and took one of his hands in hers.

'My dear Odd. Always running away. When will you turn and face what it is you're running from?'

Odd blinked in astonishment. 'I don't know what you mean. I never . . .'

He was lost for words, and he could feel the old familiar panic rising. What really made matters worse was seeing Winthropp now come in through the front door.

'Hello, Win,' he shouted cheerily, in a blatant effort to take attention away from himself.

Winthropp regarded them both and nodded solemnly:

'And the air seethes with the promise of what is to come. Another Configuration. Another glimpse into what lies beyond this tawdry reality. I've seen many. Each one a moment of grace. Each one more beautiful and more glorious than the last.'

'The advantages of age, I suppose,' said Odd. 'I wouldn't know, being so much younger than your good self.'

Winthropp didn't say anything for a moment, but, when he did speak, the word he used was almost taunting.

'Strange.'

Odd stood up and cleared his throat. He could sense Eliza tensing beside him. 'What's strange?'

'The girl. Mirabelle. So very strange. *Different*, I mean. Typical of her kind, I suppose.'

'Typical? Of her kind? Whatever can you mean?' said Odd, advancing towards Winthropp until he was only inches away from him.

'Odd,' warned Eliza.

Odd ignored her, keeping his eyes on Winthropp, searching the nebulous dark inside that hood, sensing his insolence even if he couldn't see it.

Winthropp shrugged. 'Just that.' And started to walk away.

Odd shouted after him. 'Well, Win, what can I say? Once again, it's been such a pleasure conversing with you. Your wit, your warmth, your charm.' Odd shook his head. 'You truly are a joy. One might even say a gift.'

Winthropp walked down a corridor and out of sight.

Odd roared. 'And she's *family*, Win. You'd do well to remember that. Family! More so than most because she actually understands what that word means!'

Odd looked at his hands. They were quivering, and he was trembling all over. He looked at Eliza, who was looking pityingly at him and that was when he decided, yes, she was right. So Odd did what Odd did best.

He ran.

Odd's first portal took him somewhere hot and sandy, filled with sunlight. Something moaned away to his left and he could have turned and looked, but that would have meant acknowledging he wasn't alone and he wanted to be alone.

His next took him to a forest at dusk. Birds were singing. It was beautiful. It was warm.

It was no good.

Another portal. This time a city, cold and dark and rainy, but there were people here. He could see them rushing around with their heads bowed. No good.

He kept running.

One portal after another. As if trying to outrun his rage, his sadness. Panting all the while.

He eventually slumped down on the hillside overlooking the little fishing village of which he'd become so fond in recent months. Moonlight on the water. The clink of ropes against poles, starlight speckled against the velvet dark.

His breathing returned to normal. He was finally alone.

He reached into his jacket pocket, took out a small, familiar packet of tobacco, and cradled it in his hands.

Mirabelle

Mirabelle sat with her back to Piglet's door. She could hear him whimpering to her, but she couldn't seem to find the words. When she finally did speak, her voice was hoarse.

'Mavis deserved it, Piglet. She was disrespectful.'

Piglet moaned as if in sympathy.

Lucius strutted back and forth on the floor in front of her.

'She deserved it,' Mirabelle said again, as if trying to convince herself.

There was a sound from behind Piglet's door, as if something vast had turned over and was gliding through water.

'I miss him,' said Mirabelle, wiping her eyes. 'I miss him so much. Do you miss him?'

Piglet gave an agonised moan in response.

'He was a good man. The best.'

Mirabelle couldn't stop thinking about Dr Ellenby. She'd lost someone before, but it had been different in a way because it had been her mother, whom she'd never known in the first place. This was someone she'd known her whole life. Someone she'd grown up around. Someone who'd seen her birth, known her mother. Someone who'd been her protector, even if she hadn't known it. It felt as if the pain was devouring her from the inside out. She had never felt so utterly weary.

She stood up and Lucius flew back on to her shoulder.

'They can keep their Configuration. I don't want to see it anyway.'

She headed away down the corridor, leaving Piglet behind once more.

Piglet

Piglet listens.

He listens to the air. It ripples and trembles with voices and the promise of eons-old magic. Some of the voices shriek, some whimper. There is fear. There is excitement. A tremulous anticipation. A swelling wonder.

Piglet has sensed all this before. Ages past. It's as familiar to him as the darkness is to the rest of the inhabitants in the house. They give it a name, but Piglet is beyond names, and words are nothing to him. Something in the mounting excitement pleases him, even makes him happy.

But there is something else.

It feels like the onrush of a dark tide to a familiar shore. The imminent arrival of something new and different.

And deadly.

Billy

Billy crept round the rear of the house.

There was a makeshift stable of sorts there, and a horse was whinnying softly in the darkness. There was a skittishness about it. No doubt the horse felt it too, the low hum in the air, the mounting electric crackle that might not be detectable by human senses, but that made his own hair stand on end. Billy looked this way and that, making sure he wasn't being followed. It was edging ever closer to midnight, and he knew everyone in the house would be preoccupied by the imminent ceremony.

Everyone that is except Mirabelle.

Billy had listened by a window to the confrontation in the hallway. He could hear the despair in Mirabelle's voice when she realised Enoch was serious about banning her from the Configuration. He felt sorry for her, and once again the guilt began to overwhelm him, but he couldn't afford to feel guilty – Meg was depending on him.

He held his satchel tight as he headed towards the stable and opened the door. He clicked his tongue and the horse ventured out.

Billy rubbed it between the ears. He wrapped his arms round the animal's neck and whispered to it, his nose filling with the horsey smell of it. Eventually he let the horse go and it nodded its head up and down vigorously as if agreeing with him.

Billy made soothing sounds and the horse pranced back and forth delicately for a moment and then stood stock still, except for the swishing of its tail.

'Wait here,' said Billy.

The horse nodded again as if it understood.

Billy sniffed the air, adjusted his satchel, then crept towards the house.

Odd

Odd returned straight into a milling crowd heading into the Room of Lights. Uncle Alfred almost stepped on him. Both apologised profusely to each other, then Odd was pushed aside unceremoniously by Aunt Esme, who was wriggling forward on her long slug-like tail while chattering away to another aunt.

Odd tried to keep his balance, but he bumped straight into Gideon, who grabbed him to stop him from falling.

'Exciting, isn't it?' said Gideon, smiling broadly, his single eye shining with delight.

'Yes, yes, it is,' said Odd, patting himself down, and then jerking out of the way of three people who seemed to be oblivious to his presence.

'I've never seen it. Never.'

Odd felt a little twinge of annoyance. 'Well, you are very young.'

'I wonder what it's like,' said Gideon, trying to see over people's heads while clutching Odd at the same time.

'You'll find out soon enough,' said Odd as Gideon propelled him forward.

Inside the room, people arrayed themselves around its edges in a rough circle. The room looked brighter, Odd thought for a moment. No, it *felt* brighter.

There was constant excited chatter. Some people had watches and were looking at them. In truth, they didn't need them. Everyone knew instinctively when the moment was coming.

Odd looked at the orbs. They seemed to be shining brighter. He felt a surge of excitement, and everything he'd seen and heard today was suddenly forgotten.

Someone to his left let out a yelp. Gideon pointed.

'Look!'

A large shimmering purple orb had started to revolve and was moving slowly towards a point just above the centre of the room.

'It begins,' said a familiar voice to his left.

Odd turned to see Enoch standing beside him, along with Eliza.

Mirabelle

Mirabelle sat on her window ledge, looking out over the garden. She became aware that Lucius was flapping around the room and becoming more agitated with each passing moment.

'What is it, Lucius? What's wrong?'

Lucius wheeled round the room, cawing hoarsely. Mirabelle had to duck at one point to avoid him crashing into her.

She wondered if it was the Configuration that was affecting him. She could feel it herself, like pulsing waves of energy in the air. There was a pressure in her head that alternated with a strange light-headedness.

Lucius started flying in circles round the ceiling.

Billy

As Billy made his way down the gloomy corridor, he remembered Thorne's words: *As long as they're distracted by the Configuration, they won't know. Remember what I told you. The orb must be used at precisely the right moment.*

Billy tried to ignore the tightening knot in his stomach. He could feel the strange vibrations in the air. He fought the urge to turn back and instead thought about Meg.

He turned into the larder. The smell of raw meat was strong here, but so too was the smell of metal.

He spied the key hanging from a hook on the wall. His palm was slick with sweat as his fingers closed round it.

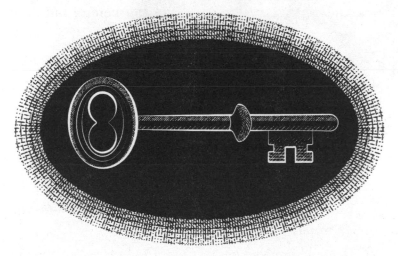

Odd

More of the orbs were spinning now, slowly, balletically, and they were gradually moving together to form a pattern that only they could understand, aligning themselves in a strange constellation of light and energy as they had done every one hundred years.

Red and gold and sapphire they shone, trembling and shimmering with light as their audience looked on in silence now, gaping in awe at the sight, knowing more was to come. Odd had seen this twice before, but this time it seemed different, like a slight melodic variation in a familiar song.

'Beautiful, aren't they?' said Eliza, the rainbow colours gliding over her face like light refracted through water.

Gideon whimpered beside Odd. Odd placed a hand on his shoulder.

'What's happening?' Gideon asked.

'No one knows,' said Odd. 'No one has ever known, but some think it shows us . . .' Odd suddenly couldn't speak. It felt as if the words were stuck in his throat. Tears welled in his eyes. There was something about the whole experience that moved him beyond words.

The orbs suddenly blazed with new brightness and people shielded their eyes and many gasped in wonder when the light faded just a little, just enough for them to see . . .

'The Ether,' gasped Odd.

Mirabelle

Lucius was now throwing himself against the closed door.

Mirabelle was stunned.

'Lucius! Stop it! Stop it!' she shouted.

He paid her no heed.

Billy

Billy stood before Piglet's door. He gently took the silver orb from his satchel and laid it on the ground. He reached into his pocket and took out the key.

He steeled himself.

Then he stepped towards Piglet's door and inserted the key in the lock.

Odd

'What is it?' Gideon asked. He was almost crying.

Odd smiled, despite the tears streaming down his cheeks. 'No one knows for certain, but some think it's a glimpse of the Ether.'

What looked like a gossamer cloud hung above the room. A small nebula of light and dark had appeared between where the spheres had been. It looked as if a veil had been drawn aside, and a separate universe complete unto itself had opened up, and within that universe could be caught glimpses of shapes not unlike people that floated through this small cosmos. Some glided alone and some merged with others, forming clouds that pulsed with light before they eventually parted to glide away, shimmering and throbbing with life. Things that looked like stars blazed in this pocket universe. Red, orange, sapphire, all cloaked in a velvet blackness that seemed to hum and pulsate with a strange life.

'What are they?' asked Gideon, pointing at the gliding shapes.

It took all Odd's strength to answer. He felt as if he were caught deep within a dream. One from which he never wanted to wake.

'Souls,' he said. 'I think they're souls.'

'They're beautiful,' Gideon said.

'You were like that once. We all were,' said Odd. 'Souls floating in the Ether, waiting to be called by the spheres, waiting to be born.'

Billy

The door was open now and something moved within the dark of Piglet's room. Something huge and hulking. Billy fought the trembling that took hold of his body as he held the orb up. He concentrated just as he'd been told to and, as Thorne had promised, the top half of the orb opened and pulled back, golden light spilling from its core.

Piglet stepped out of his room. Hot breath expelled from the nostrils of the form he had taken. A form not unlike that of a dragon, melded with something concocted of spines and claws. His feet were huge. His talons sharp and curved. His eyes burned with a fierce molten glow.

Billy stuttered.

'L-look . . . look at the light, just look at the light.'

Piglet frowned. He tilted his head.

Then he reared up on his hind legs and roared.

Mirabelle

It was when Mirabelle heard the roar that she finally opened the door. Lucius flew out into the hallway. Mirabelle felt a blind terror like nothing she'd ever known before.

She pelted after Lucius.

Odd

'Did you hear that?' asked Odd.

Gideon was too mesmerised by the light display to answer. Odd looked around him, but everyone else was similarly entranced. He was about to ask Enoch the same question.

But that was the moment he heard Piglet start howling.

Piglet

Piglet looks at the light.

There is something about it. Something soothing. Warm.

He can hear the light calling to him.

He looks at the trembling boy. The boy is speaking, but that doesn't matter to him. All that matters to Piglet now is the light.

Piglet knows he must go to it.

Piglet makes himself smaller. The light reaches out to him, like a friend. Piglet smiles.

But something . . .

Something is wrong.

Piglet recoils, but he cannot pull away. It is as if the light has teeth, and they fasten on him and the light bites down and it hurts and it burns. It hurts so, so much.

Piglet screams.

Mirabelle

Mirabelle had seen the eerie glow from the end of Piglet's corridor and she knew when she heard him scream that something terrible was happening. It was unlike any sound she'd heard him make before. It sounded as if he were in agony.

What shocked her more than anything was seeing Billy holding the silver orb between his hands while a twisting, roiling mass of light struggled to free itself from whatever magic was pulling it into the orb.

She knew instinctively that the light was Piglet.

'Stop it! Leave him alone!' she shouted as she raced towards Billy.

Lucius dive-bombed Billy, but Billy shrugged him off, too busy concentrating on the orb.

The orb closed and the light was cut off with such suddenness it felt like the final descent of a guillotine blade.

Mirabelle tackled Billy. They both hit the ground, but

somehow Billy kept his hold on the orb.

'Let him go!' Mirabelle roared.

Billy looked panicked and terrified. He kicked out, and Mirabelle was flung against a wall.

Her head cracked against it and she slumped to the floor. Through a grey haze she could see Billy standing over her. Was he crying? He was babbling something.

'. . . sorry . . . I have to save her . . . have to . . .'

Mirabelle tried to move, but it sent a shudder of pain through her skull. She closed her eyes just for a moment and, when she opened them again, Billy was gone.

Odd

Odd ran at first, before remembering he could just use his portal. It helped him outpace the other Family members.

He knew exactly where to go.

He was shocked when he saw Piglet's door open. Too many scenarios flooded his mind. Too many memories of a similar night from years ago. He saw Mirabelle slumped against a wall. He knelt before her. Her eyes were foggy. It seemed to take her a great effort to focus. Finally, she managed to grab him by the arms.

'He took Piglet. Billy took Piglet.'

Part 4
Piglet in the World

Billy

Billy held fast to the horse as it pelted through the dark. He'd cinched the satchel tight to his body, but even so it still bounced against his ribs and he could feel the weight of the orb. Maybe it was his imagination, but each time it hit him he felt as if it were hot. He shifted the satchel round to his stomach, hoping it would stop it from bouncing so much.

He saw Mirabelle's face again. That look of betrayal in her eyes. If he were honest, that look burned far more than any physical object could. He wiped the sweat from his brow and tried to vanquish the image, but it kept coming back to him. He clenched his jaws hard and gave a guttural moan of rage. He was angry with himself, sick with guilt and shame. Mirabelle had been the one person who had offered him genuine warmth and friendship at Rookhaven, and now he'd thrown it back in her face.

He tried to calm himself, but all he could manage was a great bellow of frustration. The horse neighed in fright as Billy made him pull up. He leapt off its back and started to march agitatedly back and forth, tearing at his hair. He could go back. It wouldn't be that hard. He could go back and explain. He owed her that.

We'll put her in the machine.

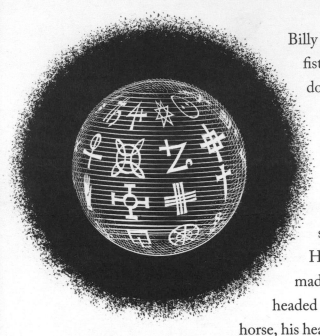

Billy clenched his fists and hunkered down, looking at the road ahead and the road behind. He could see Meg's face now. He shook his head. His decision was made for him. He headed back to the horse, his head bowed. Before he mounted it again, he felt the roundness of the orb in his satchel. For some reason, he couldn't help himself. He undid the straps and took the orb out.

It looked exactly as it had before. There was no indication that it contained anything. But it felt heavier. Did it weigh just that bit more? Had he imagined it?

He couldn't understand how such a small object could contain such a large and powerful creature. Because, make no mistake about it, Piglet was certainly powerful. He'd sensed that even when Piglet had taken the shape of a small boy. There was no mistaking the waves of power that had come off him, and the sense that he was tapped into greater, much older, energies than any other creature in that room. Just thinking about it almost made Billy's hair stand on end again.

He put the orb back in the satchel. It looked strange there beside something so ordinary as his copy of *Treasure Island*. He tied the satchel tight, then hopped back up on the horse. He stroked its neck and spoke to it gently. He had to hurry, but there was no sense in upsetting the animal. He let it trot for a moment then, with one final look behind him, he urged it into a full gallop.

Mirabelle

'Why would he do that? Why?' said Mirabelle.

A frightened-looking Odd helped her to her feet. She still felt slightly stunned.

'What happened exactly?' he asked.

'Billy had a small device,' said Mirabelle. 'It had runes on it, and Piglet was sucked into it and it sealed him in. He tried to fight it but—'

She was interrupted by a commotion from the other end of the corridor. Enoch and some other Family members were arriving. She heard someone call her name. Before she could say anything, Odd pushed her through a portal.

They arrived at the edge of the Path of Flowers. Odd held her arm and urged her to take in a deep breath.

Mirabelle took a moment, then straightened up. 'We're going after him.'

'How? We can go through as many portals as you like, but it's pointless without knowing where he's going.'

'Perhaps I can help with that,' said a voice as dry and brittle as ancient paper.

They turned to see Winthropp standing nearby.

'Really, Win? And how can you be of service?' asked Odd.

'I can track them.'

'Both Billy and Piglet?' said Odd. 'You'll hardly be able to catch Piglet's scent. He's trapped inside some kind of—'

'No, *them*. I can track them.'

Winthropp turned and looked deliberately at Mirabelle.

'He means the Misbegotten,' said Mirabelle, glaring back at him.

Winthropp gave a little supercilious nod.

'I cannot deny I have been blessed with a certain talent,' he said. 'It has its uses. I would, however, suggest that those of us who need protection from sunlight take their pendants with them. The boy has the added advantage of being able to travel during daylight.'

Odd nodded in understanding and disappeared through a portal.

'Why are you doing this?' asked Mirabelle, eyeing Winthropp suspiciously.

Winthropp shrugged. 'The creature is Family. He needs our help.'

'He's called *Piglet*. He's a member of *my* family and he's in danger – that's why *I'm* helping him. Somehow I think you might have your own reasons.'

Odd reappeared through a portal before Winthropp could reply. He handed Winthropp a pendant and patted his own chest.

'Always wear mine just in case I skip into a sunnier clime without thinking. Are we ready?'

'Yes. Let's not waste any more time,' said Mirabelle.

Billy

Billy reckoned he'd been riding at a gallop for close to an hour when he happened upon the outskirts of a large town. He thought about going around the town, but the quickest route to London (and more importantly back to Meg) was through it. The moon shone down with a whiteness that was much too brilliant for his liking. He cursed the fact that there wasn't a cloud in the sky, but he was set on his next course of action.

The horse was exhausted. Billy felt guilty about what he'd put it through. He climbed down off its back and whispered to it, thanking it for its help. Then he patted the animal and set it free.

Billy made his own way into the town. The streets were deserted, but he kept his ears pricked all the same. There wasn't a sound or a scent on the air. Billy almost felt as if he could relax.

Then he remembered the object in his satchel.

The urge to take it out and look at it was overpowering, but he resisted. If he were honest with himself, he was too afraid to do so.

Was that a low humming sound he could hear? Strange vibrations?

He put the question to the back of his mind and walked

on. Once again, he remembered the look in Mirabelle's eyes, and tried to will the image away.

He heard tinkling up ahead. He crouched low beside a row of houses and spotted the source. There was a milkman doing his rounds with his horse and cart. Billy ducked down a lane out of sight. The milkman was carrying a wire basket filled with milk bottles, and Billy could hear the almost comforting clink of glass against glass.

Billy walked the lane. He wasn't tired. He reckoned he could make London in a day or two. He stopped short for a moment in front of a toyshop window. There was a collection of mangy-looking teddy bears and a doll's house, but what caught his eye was a porcelain doll dressed in red gingham. Her skin shone and her eyes were of the brightest blue. Billy reckoned it was the kind of thing that

Meg would love. He thought about the look on Meg's face if he could bring something like that back for her. Billy laid his hand on the window and, despite all he'd been through, he somehow managed a smile.

'Would you mind telling me what you're doing?'

Billy froze for a moment. He could see a reflection in the windowpane. There was no mistaking the dark uniform or the tall hat.

He turned to look at the constable, mindful of his escape routes as he did so.

'Hello, officer,' he said, trying to sound as casual as possible.

The bobby tilted his head. 'I asked you a question.'

Billy fought the urge to lick his lips. Instead he forced a smile. 'I was just on my way to my gran's.'

'At this hour?'

Billy nodded, still smiling. He thought it was better to keep up the pretence rather than risk something that might expose him.

'What have you got in your bag?'

At this question the tingling panic he'd been feeling almost exploded, but he dampened it down and tried to restrain the urge to fight or run.

He shifted the satchel forward on his hip to give the impression of cooperation and openness.

'Nothing much, just a couple of little things.'

He was keenly aware of the weight of the orb against his hip. He'd managed to not think about it for a short time, but now it made his panic double-edged. Was it his imagination or did the orb seem hot, as if it might burn through his satchel?

'Let me see, then,' said the police officer, holding out his hand.

Billy stepped forward, although his legs felt as if they belonged to someone else. The officer nodded at the satchel. Billy undid the straps, trying again to appear as casual as possible, but he was conscious of the fact that, despite the coolness of the night, sweat had broken out on his forehead. He reached into the satchel and took out *Treasure Island*, holding it up so the policeman could see.

The policeman looked bemused. 'A book.'

'It's my favourite,' said Billy.

'And that's all you've got?'

Billy nodded.

'What's that, then?' said the policeman, nodding at the bulge in the side of the bag.

Billy, his smile feeling more than a little strained, tried to appear blasé. He opened the bag a little for the police officer to have a peek.

'It's an ornament. It belongs to my gran. My mum was polishing it up for her.'

'Give it here.'

Cold, damp dread filled Billy, suffusing his every limb. He seemed to be moving in slow motion as he reached into the bag and took the orb out. He knew in his heart of hearts that it weighed no more than it had before, but to him it felt somehow darker, denser, like a star compacted into a tiny sphere. He held it up. The officer made a beckoning gesture.

'Let me see it.'

Billy handed the orb to him and the officer gave his book back to him. Billy rammed the book back into his satchel. His heart was thudding so hard in his chest now that he could swear the officer could hear it.

The bobby held the sphere up. 'An ornament, you say?'

Billy nodded. He couldn't speak. His heart felt as if it were leaping out of his chest when the officer suddenly hefted the orb a few inches up in the air and then caught it.

'It's like a paperweight,' said the officer.

'Yes, a paperweight,' said Billy, a little too eagerly.

The officer frowned. 'Funny-looking, though.'

There was a pause as he examined the runes. Billy clenched a fist.

The officer was just about to hand the orb back when he nodded at the shop. 'Doing a bit of window-shopping, were we?'

Billy just chuckled. He held his hand out.

The officer narrowed his eyes. 'This is your gran's? You sure you haven't lifted it?'

'My gran's, yeah,' said Billy, a little too sharply. His patience was wearing thin.

'Funny time of night to be heading to hers.'

Billy shrugged.

'Where does she live, then, this gran of yours?'

It was just a flicker in the officer's eyes, just the tiniest flicker that told Billy all he needed to know. Too many years on the streets had taught him about all the subtle shifts in any confrontation, and this one had shifted the wrong way for him.

He gave an airy, expansive gesture to his left.

'She lives just . . .'

And in one swift movement he grabbed the orb and kicked the officer's legs out from under him.

Billy ran. He was hoping against hope that that would be the end of it, but the piercing shriek of the officer's whistle told him he was in a lot more trouble.

He turned back for a moment to see the bobby picking himself up off the ground, making a swipe for his helmet, which had been knocked clean off his head.

'Stop thief!' he shouted, then gave a second blast of his whistle.

Billy accelerated. He rounded a corner.

Just in time to see another police officer pelting towards him.

Billy looked around wildly. There was no other route out of the lane. The only way was up. He leapt for the nearest drainpipe, but the one he'd picked was rusty and decayed. He managed to scrabble up one-handed a couple of feet, with the orb in the other hand, but the drainpipe gave way with a screech, and he hurtled backwards on to the ground.

The second police officer was almost upon him, and the first was gaining fast, his arms and legs pumping, his face white with rage.

Billy sprang up and charged straight into the second policeman, sending him spinning into a wall. He flew out of the lane and straight on to a wide street. He ran for all he was worth, cradling the orb tight to his chest. He took a moment to look back at his two pursuers.

It was a mistake.

He hadn't heard the milkman and his horse making their way out of a side street. Billy turned and tried vainly to stop himself, but he was running too fast and he collided with the horse, which reared up in a panic. It was like hitting a brick wall.

He bounced off the horse and into the cobbled street.

The orb flew out of his hand and hopped along the cobbles.

Billy was too winded to move. He tried to crawl, but the pain in his chest was too much, and all he could do was gasp for air.

Hands grabbed him. The second police officer. The first arrived moments later, eyes blazing. Billy was lifted off the ground. The police officers roared at him. Billy couldn't really hear them. There was a ringing in his ears.

And something else.

A rumbling sound coming from behind. Billy turned to see a truck barrelling up the street.

The orb had stopped in the middle of the road, caught

in the furrow between two cobbles. Billy tried to wrench himself free. He tried to shout a warning.

The truck was bearing down on the orb.

Billy howled, the blood fizzed in his veins, his teeth elongated and he caught sight of the look of terror in one of the police officer's faces. Billy wrenched himself free, grabbed one of the officers by the midriff and flung him straight into his companion. Both men flailed backwards along the path in a tangle of limbs. Billy turned his attention back to the orb.

But it was too late. He watched in horror as the truck drove over the orb.

White light exploded from under its front wheel.

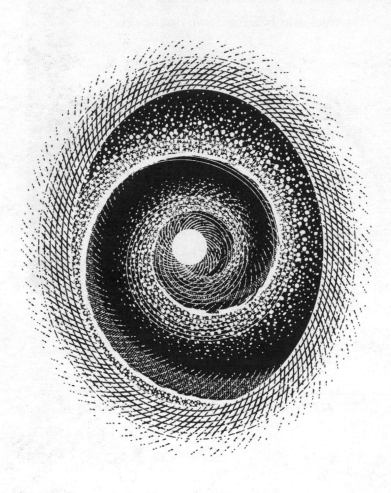

Piglet

To Piglet it feels like an unravelling.

For a while he knew only darkness, confusion, fear.

Now he expands outwards like an exploding sun. Free again. Piglet again.

He coos with delight. He can feel the moon. He hasn't felt the moon like this in an age, not since . . .

The memory escapes him, because for now there are more important and immediate matters to which to attend.

He towers over the street, sees beneath him a vehicle lying on its side, a man rushing away from its cab, gibbering in terror. Two other men in uniform help each other up off the ground. Another man scrabbles and slips along the path as he tries to steer a horse and cart away. Their fear is electric. The men scatter in different directions.

And the boy is there.

He sits looking up in abject terror as Piglet looms over him.

The boy tries to scramble away.

There are lights coming on in some of the houses. Someone screams, but Piglet doesn't care. All that interests him is the boy.

Piglet knows very little about him. Piglet is curious. He is always curious.

So Piglet plunges towards him.

Mirabelle

The three of them stepped out of a portal near the side of a narrow dirt road. Winthropp walked some of the way up the road, his head raised as if he were sniffing the air. Mirabelle called after him, but he simply ignored her.

'What's he doing?' she asked Odd.

'I have no idea,' Odd replied.

The portal was closing, and Lucius flew through it just before it winked out of existence.

'Go home, Lucius,' said Mirabelle.

He gave an insolent caw in response and settled on a tree branch above her head.

'I said, *go home.*'

'Maybe he'll be of some use,' said Odd in that placatory tone of his that Mirabelle especially despised lately. She still hadn't forgiven him for not coming to Dr Ellenby's burial.

'He won't,' said Mirabelle.

'If you say so,' said Odd.

Mirabelle clicked her fingers and pointed back in the direction of Rookhaven. Lucius cawed at her, then finally took flight and wheeled away into the sky. Mirabelle watched him until he became a tiny black speck against the moon.

'He's stubborn,' she said.

Odd cleared his throat. 'I would say he reminds me of someone, but maybe I shouldn't.'

Mirabelle shot him a withering look.

Winthropp had returned.

'I thought I'd lost the traces, but he seems to have passed this way. We should go,' he said. 'If we could travel to another point, I could get my bearings a little more.'

'Just a couple of things, Winthropp,' said Mirabelle.

Winthropp turned and regarded her coolly. 'Yes?'

'Do you know what's going on? Have you heard of a device like this being used before? And why would anyone want to take Piglet?'

Winthropp seemed to look at her for a very long time, so long, in fact, that Mirabelle found herself getting slightly irritated.

'I have no idea, and I have heard of no such device before.'

'Someone made it, though. Someone who knew about Piglet and knew how to trap him. How would they know all that? What do they want with Piglet?' said Mirabelle.

'I don't know,' said Winthropp.

Calm. He is oh so calm, thought Mirabelle. *Infuriatingly so.*

'You must have some suspicions.'

Winthropp frowned. 'Suspicions?'

'Ideas. Theories. Something.'

Winthropp looked at her blankly.

'I mean you are old, very old, so I hear. The mysterious

Winthropp. And you must know a lot being so very old and so very nosy. I mean, I've seen the way you watch other people. You never say much, but you're always watching.' Mirabelle's eyes narrowed. 'What exactly is it that you're looking for? Is it their weaknesses?'

Winthropp's demeanour changed to what she thought might be amused curiosity, as if what she was saying were somehow irrational. This only made her angrier. There was a long pause, until finally he proffered a single word.

'Interesting.'

Then he turned to Odd and started to talk about where they should exit from the next portal.

Mirabelle pushed herself between the two of them and stood inches in front of Winthropp's face.

'You suspect more than you're letting on. I can tell from your voice.'

'We really need to get moving,' said Winthropp. 'The boy has a head start on us and time is of the essence, as you know.'

Odd opened another portal. Winthropp stepped through it first, and Mirabelle grabbed Odd's arm before he could follow.

'I don't like him, Odd.'

Odd shrugged. 'He's our only way of getting Piglet back.'

They stepped into the portal and it disappeared. There was silence for a moment, then the shadow of a raven passed over the road.

Billy

Billy felt as if he'd been engulfed by a tidal wave.

Staring up at the creature that had towered above him had been terrifying enough. This was something more than what he'd encountered when Piglet had first left his room. This was a pillar of flame, of burning, turning cogs and wheels of fire and hundreds of eyes, like some living machine, and then it had descended towards him.

And then the street was gone. The world in which Billy now found himself was an ethereal space of golden clouds lit by flashes of pink, and blue, and red. He had a feeling he was being watched, studied almost, as if those eyes had become one, and that eye was examining him under a microscope.

Billy wanted to run, but it was impossible because he was . . .

Everywhere and nowhere.

The thought frightened him, because it had come unbidden and it didn't feel like his.

Billy was too terrified to move. Instead he reached out a hand.

The mist vanished.

He was in the cellar now. It was cold. Winter outside. He remembered this. He could see himself in the gloom as if he were outside his body, both here and not here.

He was crouched on the floor. He was younger. A lot younger. He'd just brought the Catchpoles something and they were jammed into a corner on their knees eating it, and he could hear meat rending and bone breaking. Dad turned round, his eyes white in the shadows, dark blood dripping down his chin.

'Billy's ever so good to us, isn't he, Mum? Ever so good for bringing us things.'

Mum didn't respond. The image rippled. Billy felt a moment of panic, but then there was something else. The sensation of being calmed, shushed somehow. The image changed completely, and now Billy could see himself and Meg in a lane. It was the evening he'd found her. He could see himself leaning down towards her. He didn't have to hear the words – he could remember them off by heart.

'I think I know what you are. You're like me, and you've been alone for a long time, but you're not alone now.'

And she took his hand, and this time the image shimmered because Billy had tears in his eyes.

And now he felt as if he were falling, and the air whistled past him and the mist became grubby whitewashed walls, and he watched again as the Catchpoles were ushered towards the machine. Images came thick and fast now. The dreadful dust, all that remained of the Catchpoles. Meg's tear-stained face. Her face again that night he'd found her. The way she smiled when he read to her. And all the time he could feel the weight of that vast presence, the sense of Piglet looking down at him, at his life, recording every moment. It was almost as if his mind were being ripped open and scoured.

And then everything changed, like the current of a river suddenly switching direction midstream.

He could see the House of Rookhaven now under the starlight. Before he knew it, he was inside, walking its corridors, listening to the voices. He saw Mirabelle talking to a bearded man who was wearing an assortment of oddly coloured clothes and a cravat. He was showing her something in a notebook. Mirabelle smiled at him.

The image rippled and now he saw Mirabelle sitting outside the door to Piglet's room and talking. The vision shimmered, and now he saw… no, that didn't sound right. He was *presented* with the image of an old well-dressed man with a doctor's bag arriving at the house. The images were hurried now. A freckle-faced girl. A pale boy in a bed, and the man with the bag sitting on the bed and checking the boy's temperature. Mirabelle and the girl sitting together on a bench near the flowers at night.

And somehow Billy knew that these were someone else's memories, images that Piglet kept within his own mind, which he was offering up to Billy now.

Then something horrid.

A shadow. A stinking clawed shadow, howling with bloodlust. Billy wanted to turn away from this vision. It seemed to blot out everything. And Mirabelle stood before it, and the air roiled around her, and then the ravens came, plummeting from the sky, and they tore that dark monstrosity to shreds. And Mirabelle's eyes burned with hunger as she devoured the black heart of what remained of the shadow.

And now he saw Mirabelle's face. Just in the moment before he betrayed her.

Billy wanted to say sorry.

But then everything vanished, and he was back on the street again.

A clump of grey mist splashed with scarlet and gold floated above him. Billy edged away from it towards the wall behind him.

The mist followed him. It floated downwards, solidified, condensed. And now Piglet was in the first form in which he'd seen him, the shape of the boy from the Room of Lights. And yet Billy could still feel the power radiating from him.

Piglet tilted his head, looking at him quizzically.

He held his hand out towards Billy.

Billy pushed himself up against the wall into a standing position.

Then he ran.

Piglet

Piglet watches the boy run away. This confuses him. He only wanted to help.

The boy's memories were fascinating, Piglet thinks about them now, going through them like the pages of a book, picking the more interesting ones.

Mirabelle's face.

The people in the cellar.

The little girl's face.

When the little girl's face appears, Piglet can feel the warmth the boy feels for her. The . . .

What is it called again?

The love. That's it. The love he feels for her.

Love.

Words. So small, so silly in their own way, but so powerful too, Piglet thinks.

And then there was Mirabelle's face in the boy's mind. It was a face the boy kept returning to over and over again. The dismay. The shock.

These expressions hurt the boy, almost like knives, and then the boy felt . . .

Guilt. That's it. The boy feels guilty now.

Guilt and love. Piglet thinks about these feelings for a moment. They are so interesting, and it seems that sometimes *they can be intertwined. Piglet has never realised this before.*

    He sees the little girl's face again, and he feels the boy's terror, his anger, his hopelessness.

    His love.

    And that's when he makes his decision.

    Piglet looks up at the moon and smiles and basks in its glow.

    Piglet likes being out in the world. He'd like to be out in it a little longer.

    And so, his decision made, Piglet walks into the night.

Billy

Billy ran, his feet pounding the pavement, panting hard enough that the sound echoed through the night.

He didn't care. He had to get away from Piglet. The mind that touched his was vast and powerful, and it could see everything.

Billy didn't like that feeling one bit. He felt as if everything were being stripped away. His life had been spent in hiding, in trying to protect Meg.

When he thought about Meg, he almost choked as a sob rose in his throat. He wiped his eyes, and careered straight into a wall and bounced off it. He tried to keep running, but his feet tangled in themselves. He stumbled, righted himself and somehow kept going. He slipped again and as he raised himself from the ground he caught sight of something that made his heart thud in his chest.

Silhouetted against the moon and perched on the corner of a roof was a raven. He saw it start to spread its wings. Billy began running, faster this time. He could sense the raven above him, tracking him. He didn't dare look up.

Instinct brought him to a row of three-storey terraced houses, foul and neglected, looming up out of the night.

Barely even thinking, Billy tore some planking off a sealed window and crawled through it into the soft, mulchy

atmosphere of a place gone to rot. It didn't take him long to find a cellar.

He careered down the stairs and huddled in a corner, clasping his knees tight to his chest.

He thought about Meg. How would he rescue her now? This thought brought on a shuddering wave of sobs.

Eventually, he calmed down and laid his head against the bricks of the wall behind him. He forced himself to think of nothing, to make himself feel as if he were not there. He tried not to think about that pillar of fire, or Meg's face. Or anything.

Moments later he was hit with the anguished realisation that his satchel and book were gone.

Mirabelle

'He's near,' said Winthropp, raising his head and sniffing the air.

They were crouched in the shadows at the mouth of a lane. After trying several portals, Winthropp had finally caught a hint of Billy's scent and tracked him to a town. Looking out, they could see an overturned truck in the middle of what looked like the high street. A man stood before it, scratching his head while talking to two police officers.

Winthropp sniffed the air. 'Close. Very close. He was nearby quite recently. We may not even need a portal.'

'Well, that's good,' Odd began before Winthropp cut him off with a raised hand.

'Pillar of fire,' said Winthropp.

'What?' said Mirabelle.

'One of the men just said something about a pillar of fire that appeared out of nowhere then vanished. Apparently, a boy was screaming at it.'

'Piglet!' exclaimed Mirabelle.

Mirabelle caught sight of something silver glinting on the ground. She scrambled forward a few inches to pick it up, making sure to remain low. It felt warm in the palm of her hand. She showed it to Odd and Winthropp.

It was a silver metal shard covered in runes.

'If I may,' said Winthropp, holding out his hand.

'It's part of the thing that Billy used to imprison Piglet – I'm sure of it,' said Mirabelle.

'Hush now,' said Winthropp, bowing his head and wrapping the claws of one hand round the fragment.

Mirabelle rolled her eyes at Odd. Her attention was caught by the low silver glow emanating from between Winthropp's claws. He seemed to be in a trance.

'What's he doing?' Mirabelle hissed.

Odd shook his head and looked at a loss to explain it.

Winthropp gave a little sigh.

'This is a piece of the device.'

'That's what I said,' said Mirabelle.

He tapped the fragment against the palm of his hand. 'This power is old, and strange. It's not something I've ever encountered before.'

'Just as a matter of interest, what *have* you encountered before?' asked Mirabelle.

Winthropp ignored her question. 'He's very close.'

'Great, but what about Piglet?' asked Odd.

Winthropp held the piece up. 'Well, I think it's safe to surmise that Piglet is no longer held within the object. There are scorch marks, suggesting an explosion of sorts. And if, as Mirabelle suspects, the pillar of fire was Piglet—'

'Then he's free!' said Mirabelle.

'Piglet in the outside world? Well, that's just marvellous,' said Odd.

'We have to find him,' said Mirabelle.

'The boy first,' said Winthropp, pocketing the fragment within the folds of his cloak.

'Piglet is family.'

'That may be, but I find it easier to track your kind.'

He didn't have to say that, Mirabelle thought, but he had, and she didn't like it. She took it as a thinly veiled insult.

'You disagree?' said Winthropp.

'What's the point of doing that? Piglet should be our priority,' Mirabelle snapped.

'I see, I see,' said Winthropp, turning away from her for a moment. He seemed to consider something, then turned back to her. 'And tell me, in terms of *priorities*, which do you think might be more important? The capture of someone who infiltrated the great House of Rookhaven, or the fruitless search for some mindless beast?'

Mirabelle clenched her fists. Odd tried to step between her and Winthropp, but Mirabelle threw him a warning look.

'A mindless beast? Is that what you think of Piglet?'

Winthropp shrugged. 'What I think of him is irrelevant. What I think of the possible damage done by one of the Misbegotten, indeed the possibility that more might follow in his footsteps, is currently of greater concern. If one has infiltrated a sanctuary, it would suggest some degree of planning. Who knows what they ultimately have in mind? We need to question the boy to find out if he is part of a wider conspiracy. Your uncle would agree, as would your aunt, as would everyone.'

With that he looked at Odd. Odd looked forlornly at her.

'It's true, Mirabelle.'

Mirabelle was furious now. 'That's just nonsense! Why would anyone even plan something like this?'

Winthropp snorted. 'Do you have any idea how your kind are treated by the members of our family outside of Rookhaven?'

'My kind? You keep saying "my kind", like I'm different.'

Winthropp tilted his head. His tone was pitying. 'But you *are*, child. You are different.'

Different. Mirabelle was beginning to get sick of hearing the word.

'Imagine what it must be like, to be cast out, to be considered inferior somehow. Imagine what kind of anger that might inspire in others, in those who are not accepted by the Family like you are. Imagine the hate that might fester, and how it would inspire some to commit acts of war against the Family. Imagine how dangerous such people could be. How many more apart from the boy are willing to do such things? What is their ultimate goal? You fought a creature that sought to destroy the Family – you of all people should know the dangers of an outside threat breaking into any one of our sanctuaries.'

Mirabelle thought about all this. She knew exactly what it felt like to be considered separate, yet also part of the Family, and there was sense in what Winthropp was saying, but she couldn't help but think about Piglet out there. Lost. Alone.

'We will find Piglet,' said Winthropp. 'But the boy must be found first, and he must be questioned.'

'And then what?' asked Mirabelle.

Winthropp just looked at her, then turned and walked out of the opposite end of the lane. Mirabelle was furious all over again. And then scared. She wasn't sure why.

'Come on,' Odd said. 'He seems to know what he's doing.'

Mirabelle followed reluctantly.

Billy

Billy sat in the dark, not sure how much time had passed, and not really caring. He stared into the blackness, cursing his senses, because he could see every contour and corner of the room he now inhabited. He craved absolute darkness, something that might cover up his shame, his cowardice. Something that might stop those visions of Meg's face appearing before him.

He bowed his head between his legs, and it felt as if every part of him ached from a pain that was more than just physical. He needed a plan. He had to get back to Meg and rescue her. But how? And then there was the problem that he might be . . .

His head snapped up. There was no mistaking it. A noise in the house above.

There it was again, a whirring, a flapping, and he could have sworn he also heard a barely restrained caw.

Mirabelle's raven had followed him here. He could imagine it flitting from room to room, its one good eye seeking him out.

Billy stood up hesitantly and held his breath. He listened hard.

Silence now.

He let out a breath and started to creep towards the stairs.

He tested the first step. It creaked slightly and Billy winced. He skipped it and stood on the second, making his way up, inch by inch. He couldn't hear anything else now except the sound of blood rushing in his ears.

Slowly, he made his way to the door. He pushed it open gently. It was slightly warped, so it gave some resistance. He winced again, sweat pouring down his brow.

There was nothing to be seen in the tumbledown hallway. Billy crept forward, being careful to avoid bits of broken wood and bricks. He made his way round the bend at the bottom of a staircase to the main hallway.

Nothing.

If the raven were still here, it was probably perching somewhere out of sight, keeping completely silent.

Billy sniffed the air. Nothing.

He breathed a sigh of relief.

A lump of darkness with two silver eyes slid elegantly from a shadowed corner.

'Found you,' said Winthropp.

Billy grabbed the banister and hoisted himself on to the stairs. Unfortunately, the step he landed on gave way, and his leg plunged right through it.

Winthropp had bounded up the stairs after him and was now mere inches away. Billy wrenched up what was left of the plank his leg had gone through and hurled it at Winthropp. It took him full in the chest, and he tumbled back down the stairs.

Billy pulled his leg free and vaulted upwards, skipping

most of the steps on his way.

Something black and nebulous appeared before him at the top of the stairs and then Odd stepped through a portal. Billy grabbed the top of the newel post next to him and used it to swing round as he launched himself into the air. He kicked Odd in the chest, his momentum keeping him swinging in a semi-circle. He heard Odd crash into a wall as his own feet touched the floor and he sprinted across the landing.

A moonbeam shone through a hole in the roof. Billy took a second to look up, because something had flickered in the beam of light and, yes, he was sure of it, that something was winged and black.

He burst through a bedroom door, almost yelping with delight when he saw the shattered window before him.

He leapt out of it and tumbled through the air, landing deftly on his feet on the abandoned street below. He was about to launch into a sprint when he heard a voice that stopped him dead in his tracks:

'STOP!'

He turned to see Mirabelle walking towards him, her face paler than usual.

'Where is he?' she hissed.

Billy couldn't move. He wanted to explain. He wanted her to understand.

'I . . .'

Images passed through his mind. A girl with red hair, a boy standing beside her. Lights and swirling stars, and an angry mob of people marching up the Path of Flowers, and Mirabelle standing pale and serene in the moonlight . . .

Billy shook his head. 'Stop it,' he said.

Mirabelle advanced on him, her hands rigid by her sides. 'I won't. Tell me where Piglet is.'

Billy raised a hand, but the images kept coming. 'I wasn't talking to you . . . I was . . .'

A cloud of ravens exploding up into the night sky. A pair of grey eyes. The House of Rookhaven. A shadow looming over it.

Billy shook his head violently, like a wild animal, and roared. He turned to run.

A wall of silver fire suddenly erupted before him. It looked like fire, but it was cold and searing, and even from a few feet away he could feel its icy burn.

Billy turned back, but another wall of silver fire blocked his way. He could only just see Mirabelle through it.

'Stay right where you are.'

It was Winthropp. Billy could see him standing a few feet away, silver flames dancing in the palms of his upturned clawed hands.

Billy roared again and leapt towards him, but Winthropp flung his hands out and silver fire gushed from them, and now Billy found himself encircled by a ring of flames. He paced back and forth in agitation, looking for an opening, but there was none. He tensed to leap, but he saw Winthropp wag the finger of one hand at him, while cradling a silver ball of flame in the other.

'I'll let you out if you promise to behave,' said Winthropp.

'Do as he says,' said Mirabelle.

Billy was surprised by the note of concern in her voice. Their eyes locked for a moment, then he saw her face harden, as if she'd suddenly remembered his betrayal. It felt as if he'd been punched and the wind was knocked out of him. He stopped pacing and lowered his head. Winthropp nodded.

He motioned with his hands and the flames dwindled, then vanished entirely. Even though they were gone, Billy could still feel their sharp, icy sting in the air.

Winthropp raised one hand. 'You might think about making a run for it. I would advise against it,' he said.

A portal opened beside Mirabelle, and a wincing Odd stepped through it, rubbing his chest.

'Have I missed anything?' he said.

Mirabelle

Mirabelle wanted to shake Billy, shake him to his very bones, but even as she stood over him she felt a sudden pang of pity. He hunkered down looking hunted, rubbing his arm agitatedly. Mirabelle dampened down her pity and felt her fierceness return as she remembered the task at hand.

'What have you done with him? What have you done with Piglet?' she said.

Billy looked lost. 'I didn't . . . I wouldn't . . .'

She could see he was trying his best to avoid her gaze, but suddenly he looked at her as if seeing her for the first time.

His eyes widened. 'You ate it and you felt its power. You thought it was like swallowing a storm, lightning and thunder and fury, and it made you feel . . .'

Mirabelle flinched. Billy fell to his knees, clutching his head and shouting.

'He showed me so many things. I saw everything, and he saw . . . he saw *me*!' he wailed.

Mirabelle quickly checked Odd and Winthropp. They were too engrossed in what Billy was saying to take any notice of her. She took a moment to compose herself, trying to cobble together more of that fierceness, but what

Billy had said had shaken her.

'Where is he now?' she asked.

'I don't know,' said Billy.

'Why did you take him?' asked Odd.

'They have Meg. They said they'd kill her if I didn't do what they told me.'

'Who?' said Winthropp.

'A man in London.' Billy shook his head as if to clear it. 'He's rich. His name is Courtney.'

'Who's Meg?' asked Mirabelle.

'She's my sister,' said Billy hoarsely.

'They wanted you to steal Piglet?' asked Odd.

'Yes,' said Billy. He was clutching his head now, as if it might explode.

'Why?' asked Winthropp.

'I don't . . . I think . . .' Billy tottered forward, then back, before collapsing on to the ground.

Odd went to him and touched his forehead.

'He's burning up. What's wrong with him?' he asked.

'Piglet. Piglet spoke to him and I think it was too much for him,' said Mirabelle. 'Remember how weak Tom was for days afterwards?'

Billy's eyes fluttered open for a moment, and he grabbed Mirabelle's arm.

'Your raven . . . he found me,' he gasped.

Mirabelle looked up to see a raven perched on the corner of a roof, silhouetted against the moon.

'I told you to go home,' she shouted.

Lucius just sat there looking imperiously into the night.

'He was only trying to be helpful,' said Odd.

Mirabelle grunted.

Billy's arm went limp and his eyes closed again.

'We should move somewhere safer,' said Winthropp. 'I suggest the forest.'

He and Odd hoisted Billy up between them. Odd opened a portal and, just before they all stepped into it, Mirabelle looked up at Lucius again.

'Home,' she shouted.

He didn't move.

'Home, Lucius,' she said again.

He gave a squawk of protest before taking flight. Mirabelle watched him as he flew away, and just for a moment she paused at the edge of the portal and frowned as the moonlight glinted off his wings.

Piglet

Piglet wanders.

The night is dark, but filled with soft, comforting sounds. An owl hooting, badgers scrabbling through the undergrowth for food. Somewhere a fox snuffles by a tree then stops and pricks up its ears when it senses him passing.

Piglet smiles. He likes it out here. He likes the form he has taken too. At first he flew, taking on the shape of a falcon, enjoying the night air and the sensation of the world scudding past below him. But then he felt the urge to change again. Now he is content, although he doesn't know why. He looks at the hands and then at the legs that propel him forward. He could fly again possibly, or he could crawl, or he could become mist and float through the air, but somehow this form feels right for what he must do.

For a very long time, Piglet has felt aimless and adrift, content to stay where he must, even though his curiosity is boundless. But things have changed. Things are different since his mind met Billy's.

Because Piglet has a purpose now.

For a moment, images pass through his mind. He is racked by feelings that are not his own, but though these feelings belong to someone else, they are no less painful.

He sees eyes. Soft eyes. And darkness. And light.

And something harsh and metallic that thrums with power.

Yes, Piglet has a purpose now.

And nothing will stop him from fulfilling it.

Mirabelle

They set up camp in a small clearing. Winthropp suggested binding Billy, so Odd did a quick trip through a portal to fetch some rope and they used it to tie Billy to a tree.

Mirabelle sat across from Billy feeling a mixture of anger and guilt. His head sagged on his shoulder, and while he had no physical scars there was something bruised and broken about him. Again, she tried her best to deaden any pity she felt for him by remembering what he'd done.

That only made her think of Piglet, now out in the world exposed to who knew what. As old as he was, Piglet was a child in many ways, and like a child he could be too trusting. There were other dangers too. In a couple of hours, it would be dawn. They had the protection of their pendants, but Piglet didn't.

'You're thinking about Piglet, aren't you?' said Odd, sitting casually against a tree.

Mirabelle nodded. 'It won't be long before it's morning. What if he gets caught out in the sunlight?'

'You shouldn't worry. Piglet has more sense than to go out in the light. If anything, it's an advantage for us,' said Odd, wiggling his pendant between his fingers.

'I wouldn't be so sure,' said Winthropp.

'And why's that?' asked Mirabelle.

'Piglet is different.'

That word again, the one she was starting to hate. 'Oh, really, and how is Piglet different?'

Winthropp shrugged. 'He just is.'

Mirabelle narrowed her eyes. 'How would you know? Piglet is Family. I've known him all my life.'

'Are you claiming the special advantages of seniority again, Win?' Odd said.

'I am old – that's true. And being as old as I am confers certain advantages,' said Winthropp.

'And I presume special *knowledge* is one of those *advantages?*' sneered Mirabelle.

'I know this: Piglet can't be harmed by sunlight.'

She was about to ask him where he'd acquired his specialist knowledge about Piglet when a moan caught her attention.

Billy was stirring. At first his eyes rolled in his head, but then a clarity seeped into them, and he strained at his bonds with a sudden, startling fierceness.

Winthropp sighed. 'Please stop.'

Billy looked at his captors, and Mirabelle saw the flicker of panic on his face when his eyes alighted upon her. She felt that mixture of anger and pity once again.

Winthropp rose. 'I think you need to answer some quest—'

'Oh, shut up!' Mirabelle snapped, leaping to her feet and going towards Billy.

'You need to explain yourself,' she said. 'Where's

Piglet? Why did you take him?'

Billy strained at the rope. 'Let me go. I need to go!'

'Go? Go where?'

'I need to get back to her!'

'Meg? Your sister?'

Billy nodded furiously. 'Let me go.'

Mirabelle knelt down before him. 'Why did they make you steal Piglet?'

'This man Courtney, he has a machine that . . .' Billy struggled for a moment, as if he couldn't find the words. 'It extracts the essence of people. I think he wants Piglet's essence. I think it can help him live longer or something.'

Mirabelle was shocked by this. The idea filled her with revulsion, and she exchanged an anxious look with Odd.

'Their essence?' Winthropp said.

'Have you come across anything like this before, Winthropp?' Odd asked.

'Never. This is unheard of.'

Mirabelle was surprised to hear what sounded like a note of fear in Winthropp's voice. It made her even more troubled.

'They said they'd put Meg in the machine if I didn't do what I was told. They put the Worms in, and . . .'

'Worms?' said Mirabelle.

'The Catchpoles, the people who took me in. They were outcasts, and they took me in, and he put them in the machine and then they . . .'

He twisted his head away for a moment and closed

his eyes, breathing furiously through his nostrils. Then he looked at Mirabelle with anguish.

'I have to get Meg back! I have to go or they'll kill her too.'

'What was the plan? After you'd stolen Piglet?'

'I had to bring him to someone, to a meeting point, and they said they would hand Meg over there if I gave them Piglet.'

Mirabelle looked at him for a moment, as if calculating something, then she suddenly bent down and started to untie his rope. Odd stepped forward.

'Mirabelle, don't!'

The rope went slack. Billy looked at her with disbelief. She was inches from his face, glaring at him.

'You betrayed my trust, and now you're going to make amends.' Still glaring at him, she said, 'Winthropp, you can detect *our kind* as you call us?'

'Correct.'

'And Billy here, he has quite refined instincts too. Isn't that right, Billy?'

Billy looked suspicious.

'You can track things too, can't you, Billy? In fact, I think you might be able to track just about anything. Am I right?'

Mirabelle stood up as he nodded.

'Billy here is going to help us find Piglet.'

Odd

'Right, we have to keep moving,' said Mirabelle. 'Odd.'

Odd bristled a little at the presumption that he would instantly open a portal to wherever it was Mirabelle wanted to go. In his opinion, he had spent a little too much time in recent weeks escorting people and various bits of luggage back and forth between one sanctuary and another. Sometimes he regretted ever having let family members travel with him for the first time five years ago, but then again needs must – it was a time of crisis, after all, and he was, if not happy to do it, at least content knowing it had a purpose.

'I need a destination,' he said, trying to smile. He had to remind himself why Mirabelle was so angry and focused. She'd lost Piglet not long after losing Dr Ellenby. She was hurt and grieving. He understood her pain. Just thinking about Marcus gave him an awful ache in his chest, and now he too feared for Piglet's safety.

Mirabelle pointed away to her right. 'Billy thinks he went in that direction.'

Odd made a face. 'Well, that's rather vague.'

'If I can get out on the open road for a bit, maybe I can get a better sense of where he went,' said Billy.

'Well then, it's best that we move quickly,' said

Winthropp, already walking on ahead.

'Couldn't you just make a portal, Odd?' said Mirabelle.

Odd could feel his temper rising. He was about to say something, but Winthropp cut across him.

'I do believe it might be best to do as the boy says,' said Winthropp. 'After all, the portal magic may well interfere with his tracking abilities, and it's probably best to ascertain whether we can pinpoint a more direct way to intercept Piglet. As the crow flies, so to speak.'

As if on cue, there was flapping in the trees above them.

Odd would normally have smiled at the contiguity of it, but right now the forest felt surprisingly dark, even to him, and the mood too tense.

'Well then, lead the way,' he said, waving Billy forward.

Billy moved on, while Mirabelle squinted up into the trees, catching a brief glimpse of the raven. Odd could see the irritation on her face as she shook her head in annoyance at Lucius. She groaned in exasperation and fell into step with Odd as he followed Billy and Winthropp up

a slope that led towards the road.

Odd was aware of Lucius swooping down through the branches and settling himself on a tree stump.

'I thought I told him to go home,' Mirabelle hissed by Odd's ear.

Odd shrugged and muttered, 'Maybe he just doesn't like being told what to do. I can sympathise with that.'

Mirabelle gave him another of her withering looks, then turned and headed towards Lucius.

'Wait up,' Odd called to Winthropp and Billy. They turned back for a moment. 'We have a reluctant raven to contend with.' Odd tried his best to sound more jovial than he felt. He followed Mirabelle.

Lucius cawed. It was a wet, almost sticky sound in the night, quite unlike any sound Odd had heard him make before.

Mirabelle stood frozen before the tree stump.

Lucius cawed again, then flew up from the stump, flapping his wings and calling down to Mirabelle as she took a step backwards.

'Odd?' she said.

He felt a tingle of unease. Lucius flew above them, uttering that dreadful throaty call.

'Before we went through the portal, I thought I saw something when I shouted at Lucius,' said Mirabelle.

'What did you see?'

'His feathers looked different, but I just thought it was a trick of the moonlight.'

Silver light blazed in the night. Flames danced in the palms of Winthropp's hands. They threw enough light on the scene to confirm their suspicions.

'That's not Lucius,' said Mirabelle.

Odd could see now that the raven that hovered above them had two sighted eyes, unlike Lucius's one. It also wasn't feathered black, but a strange mixture of brown and dirty white. In all other respects it looked like a regular raven. But there was no mistaking the fact that there was an implicit threat in its cawing.

Billy started to sniff the air, his head darting back and forth. He tugged on Winthropp's arm and pointed into the darkness beyond their circle of light. Odd went cold as he saw at least three figures picking their way through the trees towards them.

The raven continued to flap menacingly above them. Winthropp signalled for them all to gather closer together.

Someone chuckled. It was a sound dripping with malevolence.

A tall lank-haired man wearing a leather jacket stepped out from behind a tree.

'What happened, boy? Did you forget our deal? I don't remember saying you could make friends.'

'That's him! That's Thorne!' Billy shouted.

The raven landed on Thorne's shoulder. Thorne grinned at them, and Odd could now clearly see the figures of the three men who had emerged from the undergrowth to confront them.

Winthropp threw his hands out and silver fire shot towards Thorne, filling the forest with frantic dancing shadows.

The man somehow caught the flame, condensed it into a white-hot ball of fire between his hands and threw it straight back at Winthropp.

It hit him in the chest and sent him flying backwards. Ripples of energy were flung outwards in its wake and Odd was knocked off his feet, along with the others.

Odd tumbled over and over in the air before hitting the ground. He was winded for a moment. He raised himself groggily and it seemed to him as if everything was moving in slow motion now. He'd been standing close to Winthropp and as a result had been thrown almost as far as him. He could see Mirabelle looking back at him, calling his name, as she tried to stand. He could see that Billy had recovered already, but was clearly trembling with rage and fear. The men were getting closer to Mirabelle and Billy, and Thorne was advancing towards them too, his raven flapping and cawing insolently upon his shoulder. Billy leapt at the tall man, but someone had thrown a net through the air, and now Billy was struggling against it. He was surrounded by men with cudgels and they slowly hemmed him in.

Thorne loomed over Mirabelle now. He blew something soft and powdery from the palm of his hand, and Odd watched in horror as Mirabelle gracefully fainted dead away.

A couple of feet away from Odd, Winthropp was

struggling to stand. Odd saw the gleam in Thorne's eyes as he turned his attention towards them.

Odd didn't think twice.

He scrambled to his feet, wheezing and clutching his chest.

He stumbled forward, grabbing a tottering and dazed Winthropp by the arm.

And he dragged him into a portal.

Piglet

During the night, Piglet felt strange tremblings on the air, vibrations that seemed to emanate from far away. They were buzzing and fizzing about his head, clouding his mind. He felt somehow drawn towards them, and found he almost had to struggle to resist. Eventually, the sensations stopped, and now all is calm as he stands by the side of a road and looks upon something he hasn't seen in quite some time.

Sunlight.

Piglet thinks he remembers this from a long time ago.

He looks at the light spreading across the sky, at how it dissolves away the inky black, turning it to grey and then blue. He stands under the shelter of a tree. The world is lively now, filling up with more sounds, chirrups and whistles and murmurings. Piglet remembers a time of many turnings ago, a time . . .

But the memory goes. He tries to catch it, like a child trying to catch a dandelion clock, but the breeze takes it away, away into . . .

Sunlight.

Piglet steps into it, feels its warmth, almost embraces it, then continues on his way.

He puts the strange tremblings of the previous night to the back of his mind. He remembers what Mirabelle said to him.

'Concentrate. You have to concentrate, Piglet.'

Piglet nods and concentrates on the road before him.

There is life ahead. A bustle and a quivering. The whisperings of those waking somewhere in the distance.

People. Lots and lots of people.

Piglet can't wait to meet them.

Part 5
The Pied Raven

Mirabelle

The cold breeze was like a slap to the face. Mirabelle could feel wood and sawdust against her cheek. The smell of the sawdust was particularly damp and sour, as if it had been dipped in something noxious. She tried to raise her head, but pain juddered through it, and she felt nauseous.

'It's easiest if you move slowly,' said someone from behind her.

She eventually managed to raise her head and turn, although it took a huge effort.

Billy was sitting with his back to a wall. There was a shuttered window above his head. He had dark circles under his eyes and he looked pale and drawn. He licked his lips and swallowed, then raised his arm slowly. There was a dull silver cuff on his wrist. It was covered in runes.

'Whatever you do, don't try to take it off.'

Mirabelle felt the pressure on her own arm. She rolled up her sleeve to see the same type of cuff. Instinctively, she clawed at it in an effort to remove it.

The pain between her eyes was blinding. She felt as if she'd been struck by lightning. Her body went rigid and she spasmed on the floor for a moment, then lay still, breathing hard, trying to focus on the ceiling above her.

Billy crawled towards her. She surmised that he'd had much the same experience she'd just had.

'They took us here in a van, but I'm not sure where we are.'

Mirabelle sat up. She looked around the room. It was small and grubby. There was a bench by the wall nearest the door. It had various metallic bits and bobs on it, along with an assortment of milky-looking glass flasks, measuring tubes and a mortar and pestle. There were runes scratched in the whitewashed wall above the bench in what looked like charcoal. There was a wooden table in the centre of the room, a chair and, by the other wall, a sink and a grubby sideboard. She carefully examined the cuff on her wrist. She traced the runes with her finger.

'I think he uses the runes to lay some kind of binding spell on them,' said Billy.

'He?'

The door opened and in strode Thorne. He was followed by the raven, which landed on a shelf above the sink. It was daylight outside, and with the sun streaming in through the slats in the window she could see the bird's strange brown and cream plumage clearly. It looked at her now and she returned its gaze.

'That's Abelard. Did a nice job of tracking you, didn't he?' said Thorne. He sat in the chair with his legs stretched out and his hands behind his head.

Abelard cawed, and Thorne gave Mirabelle and Billy a self-satisfied grin. Mirabelle glared at him to show she wasn't intimidated, but that just made the man's grin all the broader.

He fished in his jacket pocket and took out an apple, then deftly produced a small knife from the sleeve of his coat like a magician doing a magic trick. He began to peel the apple, letting the peel fall, then he started to cut pieces off it and throw them on to the floor for Abelard to snatch up and gobble.

Thorne pointed at Billy with his knife.

'You were supposed to do a job for me. There was the small matter of acquiring something. Now, where is it?'

'I don't know,' Billy mumbled.

'You don't know,' said Thorne. 'Is that what you'll tell your sister right before we put her in the machine? You don't know?'

Billy made to leap, but it was as if an invisible hand pushed him right back down. He could barely move. Mirabelle watched with concern as cold sweat broke out on Billy's forehead. He planted his palms on the floor and trembled, as if fighting the urge to be sick.

'Do you like them?' said Thorne.

'Like what?' growled Mirabelle, refusing to be cowed.

She noticed the flicker of mild surprise on Thorne's face. He got up from his chair and strode towards her, bending down on one knee while taking her by the forearm. Mirabelle tried to pull her arm away from him, but Thorne held fast, looking amused by her attempt. He rolled up her sleeve and tapped the cuff with his knife.

'Your clamps. Do you like them? Good, aren't they? I put a lot of work into these. You can try and stand with them, but I wouldn't recommend trying to walk more than an inch or two. They'll make you more than a little queasy.' He scratched his stubbly cheek. 'Made by request, they were. Haven't had much use for them recently. You should both be honoured.'

Mirabelle managed to wrench her arm free and Thorne guffawed and ruffled her hair. She shook her head in disgust. Thorne laughed even harder and went back and lounged in his chair. He eyed them both for a few moments.

'What should we do with them, Abelard?'

Abelard cawed.

Thorne leaned forward and pointed at Billy again. 'This one needs to make amends.' He pointed at Mirabelle. 'This one here –' he shrugged – 'maybe she can go in the machine. Don't know what it would do, though, what with her being like you,' he said to Billy. 'Mightn't hurt to try and find out.'

'I'd like to see you try,' said Mirabelle.

She held Thorne's gaze. He cocked his head at Abelard.

'See this one here, Abelard? She doesn't flinch. I admire that.'

'I haven't forgotten what you did to the Catchpoles,' said Billy, his voice thick with emotion.

Thorne snorted. 'What? Did you think they were family?'

'Shut up, shut up!' Billy shouted.

'They were outcasts for a reason, boy. The worst of their

kind. You think they spent their time scrabbling in the dark because they wanted to? No, they broke the Covenant: they hunted humans and they paid for it.'

'He has a name,' said Mirabelle.

Thorne frowned at her. 'What?'

'He has a name. He's called Billy.'

Thorne smirked. 'You know what, I should have made a special clamp for your mouth.'

'Who *are* you?' asked Mirabelle.

Thorne pretended to be taken aback. 'You're asking *me* questions now?'

'What's wrong? Are you afraid to say?'

'Do I look afraid?' Thorne said, throwing his head back and laughing.

Mirabelle advanced slowly towards him despite the fact that the effort made her feel nauseous.

'It's a simple question. Why can't you answer it?'

Thorne appraised her coolly now, then stood up and went to the bench behind him. He picked up a flask and turned it around in his hands.

'Did you like the concoction I used on you in the forest? Took me years to get the right mix. I used it on the boy too. Very effective.' He ran his hand along the runes on the wall and smiled to himself. 'I work on lots of things in here. Mostly stuff I use to catch them. I'm good at it. Catching them. I make traps. Good ones. None of those regular traps, bear traps, that kind of nonsense.' He snorted. 'My traps are works of proper craftsmanship.' He pointed at

Mirabelle and Billy. 'Clamps are good, but clamps are easy.'

'You're good at your job, then?'

Thorne leaned against the wall and tapped the flask with his nails. 'The best. I made that device that captured your friend.'

'The orb?'

Mirabelle could see that Thorne had sensed her anger and he was enjoying it.

'That's right. Good work if I do say so myself. No one's ever done that before as far as I know.' He grinned maliciously.

'Piglet's not just a friend,' said Mirabelle. 'Piglet's family.'

Thorne's face darkened. He looked furious now. 'Family? You think what you have is *family*? Skulking in your big house while the world moves on around you? You lot aren't family. What you have is obscene, disgusting. Family? Don't make me laugh.'

'So speaks a man who's probably never had one.'

Thorne flung the flask across the room where it smashed against the wall. Mirabelle refused to flinch. Now it was her turn to smile.

Thorne stomped towards her and jabbed a finger in the air.

'You know nothing. You deserve to go in the machine. That idiot Aspinall would love that. He can write up his observations in his little book. But before that I have a use for you.'

'Really?' said Mirabelle, her tone light. She reminded

herself that she'd faced worse than this man, and it was clear now that she'd rattled him. For all his bravado, he was clearly hiding something about himself.

'Your friend here may have made a mess of things, but I'm going to lay a new trap, and *you're* going to be the bait.'

Abelard cawed and flapped his wings. Thorne looked at him and gave a stupid, childish smile. Mirabelle reckoned he wasn't half as clever as he thought he was.

He turned on his heel and left the room with Abelard alighting on his shoulder.

'You shouldn't have done that,' said Billy, still wincing from his efforts to move.

'Why not?' asked Mirabelle.

'You made him angry.'

Mirabelle looked at the door.

Good, she thought.

Odd

'It's nice here, isn't it, Win? Quiet. Peaceful.'

Odd looked out over the fishing village and listened to the gentle clinking he enjoyed so much. He peered up at the light of the moon and closed his eyes for a moment, taking in a deep breath and letting it out.

'I like to come here and contemplate things. To be honest, it's a bit of a refuge for me.' He made a face. 'Which is kind of ironic because I travel to so many different places and, as someone a little more astute than I once commented, it's perhaps because I'm hiding from things.' Odd ran his fingers through the blades of grass that were by his feet. 'What do you think, Win? Do you have any thoughts on the matter?'

He turned and looked over his shoulder to where Winthropp lay splayed out on the grass. He'd been like that since they'd come through the portal. He hadn't moved or regained consciousness in the half hour since they'd arrived.

Odd turned his attention back to the village below.

'I wouldn't say I'm hiding from things, per se. Hiding's too strong a word for it. I suppose I'm probably just looking for breathing space, you know. Just to get some distance and time to think.'

A gentle breeze ruffled his hair. Odd listened to the

lapping sounds of the water. He sighed.

'A friend of mine told me about this place. He said he used to come here when things got too much for him. I meant to thank him, but—'

'Please. Just please stop talking.'

Odd leapt up and went towards Winthropp. 'You're alive!'

Winthropp sat up and clasped his hooded head between his hands.

'Where are we?' he said hoarsely.

Odd grinned. 'One of my favourite places. I never caught the name. I suppose I like the mystery. So, I'm not exactly sure where we are.'

'How delightful.'

'Or when.'

Winthropp tilted his head in curiosity.

Odd started to fiddle with his fingers. 'Sometimes I like to . . . I like to break out from the norm a little and travel to a different pocket of time.'

There was a strained silence as Winthropp seemed to study him.

'I mean I can go into the past. I tend not to do it too often. There was a point once where I thought it might be useful, you know, if I returned and influenced things, but apparently if you go with that express intention in mind time pushes back and you get catapulted back to your point of origin. It's like an elastic.' Odd made a ridiculous '*boing*' sound and gave an awkward chuckle.

Winthropp kept looking at him. Odd wasn't sure whether it was in disbelief or fascination – or maybe a bit of both – seeing as he could only make out his eyes.

'I mean, I can go back and observe things. And I can bring people with me and we can observe things. Unless it was like that one time when I brought Mirabelle to see her mother, which apparently she had done already, and yet she also hadn't . . . It's a hard one to explain.' He gestured around him. 'Take this, for instance. This is a very specific moment. Any minute now, you'll hear an owl hooting and then—'

'You're babbling,' said Winthropp, standing up and brushing himself down while looking out over the village.

'Right, sorry,' said Odd, looking at the ground.

'We need to get back.'

'Yes,' said Odd, suddenly feeling terribly guilty for leaving Mirabelle behind.

'Why did you bring us here?'

Odd shrugged. 'Instinct, perhaps. It was the first place I thought of.'

'A refuge,' said Winthropp, now walking away from him.

Odd waited for a moment then followed him.

'I should have taken us back to Rookhaven.'

'What good would that have done?'

Odd felt slightly offended. 'Well . . .'

'Your family would have been useless in this matter.'

'Well, what do *you* think we should we do?' Odd

asked, trying to keep pace with him.

'We need to find Piglet,' said Winthropp.

'What about Mirabelle?'

'Yes, I suppose.'

Odd felt a little flicker of anger. 'You suppose?'

Winthropp shrugged. It was a gesture that just fanned the flames of Odd's anger.

'She's family. She's my sister.'

'Sister? What a quaint concept. Family, yes,' said Winthropp.

'Well then,' Odd spluttered.

Winthropp just looked at him again and Odd felt the unfamiliar urge to punch him in the face.

If indeed he has a face, he thought.

Instead, he did the next best thing and opened a portal.

'Where are you going now?' asked Winthropp.

'To find Mirabelle.'

'Do you know where she is?'

Odd clenched and unclenched his hands by his sides while avoiding Winthropp's gaze.

'I don't,' he conceded.

He closed the portal. There was a long pause. Odd tried to listen to the lapping water, but his mind was a flurry.

'What happened back in the forest,' said Winthropp. 'I have never encountered anyone quite like that before. He used an arcane magic. Interesting.' He sniffed the air. 'I can pick up traces of the Catchpole boy. We can follow those. There may be several stops, although I think they may well be mere forks in the road before our ultimate destination.'

'Which is?'

'London, of course. We will find this gentleman who seems to have such a hold over the boy. Find him and we find Mirabelle.'

Odd finally felt a sense of relief. Winthropp gave him the general directions for a place he said would be 'a necessary detour' and Odd opened a portal. Before they stepped into it, Winthropp took one last look at the village and the ocean.

'Interesting,' he said.

Odd rolled his eyes.

And they left.

Mirabelle

'I'm sorry,' said Billy.

Mirabelle was trying her best not to pay him any attention. Instead, she was fighting the waves of nausea as she moved as slowly around the room as she could without her head juddering in agony. She was looking through Thorne's jumble of discarded bits of metal, wood and test tubes. She'd already discovered to her cost that walking too close to the door meant risking a paralysing bout of pain.

'Sorry,' she said, 'about what?'

'Everything,' said Billy. 'I'm sorry I lied to you. I'm sorry I took Piglet.'

She turned to him, wanting to be angry. But, looking at him now, she felt pity resurface. He looked lost and broken. She tried to quell the feeling.

I will not feel sorry for you. I will not.

'I had to do it for Meg. You'd have done the same if it was Odd.'

'Stop trying to defend what you did!' She didn't want to admit it, but he was right. She would have done it for Odd.

'I found her years ago. She was like me. She's like *us*.'

Mirabelle picked up a pan, then discarded it. 'You mean Misbegotten?'

'Yes.'

'Stupid word,' Mirabelle muttered. She pulled at a drawer. It was stiff and old, almost painted shut. She managed to get it open, and her eyes fell on an old nail. It was long and fortunately not rusted. She picked it up and smiled.

'You'd have done it for Jem.'

Mirabelle rounded the table a little too suddenly with the nail clenched in her hand. She had to fight a wave of clamp-induced sickness, but she managed to get the words out.

'And how would you know that?'

Billy looked suitably guilty. 'Because of the way you spoke about her. And what Piglet showed me.'

That look of guilt again. Billy looked helpless. Mirabelle realised he was only looking out for his sister. She could at least understand that. She sat down slowly in front of him and sighed.

'You miss her,' he said.

'Yes,' said Mirabelle, picking at the floorboards with the nail.

'I know what that feels like.'

No, you don't, Mirabelle wanted to say, but she knew it wasn't true.

'You miss Dr Ellenby too.'

Mirabelle shook the nail at him. 'Don't you dare say his name. Don't you dare.'

She turned her face away and swallowed hard.

'He was a good man,' said Billy.

'How would you know?'

'Because Piglet showed me.'

'Lovely. Did Piglet show you *everything*?'

There was silence for a moment.

'I'm sorry,' said Billy.

'You said that already.'

'I'm not looking to be forgiven.'

'Don't worry – you won't be.'

'But I am sorry. I thought we could be friends. You were kind to me.'

'I was stupid.'

Billy shook his head.

'Give me your arm!' Mirabelle demanded, wanting to shut him up. When Billy didn't respond, she grabbed his arm and then dug her hands under the rim of the clasp and pulled.

Within seconds, she was laid out on the floor, her temples pounding with a grey, nauseous pain. She turned to see that Billy was in almost the exact same position as her. It was an effort for her to speak.

'Right . . . I thought . . . I just had an idea that if we couldn't take our own clasps off that maybe . . .'

Billy screwed his eyes shut and shook his head slowly.

'Right,' Mirabelle gasped.

It took a few more seconds for her to recover. She sat herself up, a dull thudding still pulsing in her brain.

'I did have another idea,' she said. She held up the nail and then tapped it on her clasp. 'I've seen Enoch use runes before, and let's just say these clamps only work because of the runes. If you change them, they lose their power.'

Billy didn't look convinced. Mirabelle didn't feel too convinced either, but she clung to the idea anyway. They had to try to escape somehow.

'If I use it on yours first,' said Mirabelle, 'maybe if there's any reaction it won't be as bad.'

'You want to scratch the runes off?' said Billy.

'Even just defacing them might be enough.'

She motioned for him to put his hand forward. He did as she signalled, and Mirabelle wrapped her hand round his clamp. She looked at him, and the words were out of her mouth before she could stop herself.

'I'll help you find her. I promise.'

Billy nodded at her in appreciation. Mirabelle didn't want to give him the satisfaction that she might have relented in some way, so she still glared at him as a sign that he wasn't forgiven.

She grasped the nail in her fist and held the point firmly against Billy's clamp. She started to push down.

'Wait!' said Billy.

He held his hand out. 'I can do it better. I'm stronger.'

Mirabelle handed him the nail and she rolled up her sleeve. Billy held the nail in place. He locked eyes with her.

'Ready?'

'Ready.'

Billy drove the nail in and down. There was a moment when Mirabelle felt as if something inside her skull had splintered. It was a feeling that was gone almost before she could register it fully, then there was a clicking sensation. She instinctively closed her eyes.

When she opened them again, she looked at the clamp. The runes had a jagged line running through them, and a subtle golden vapour was rising from the metal and melting in the air. A groaning Billy was lying on the floor in front of her with one hand clasped to his head. The nail was lying in the palm of his other outstretched hand.

Mirabelle looked at him lying there, and then something occurred to her.

She could leave him there. She could just get up and leave, and there was no way he could follow her because the clasp would do its magic and prevent him from doing so.

Billy continued to groan. Mirabelle looked at him, feeling herself tensing.

She took the nail from his hand and grasped his arm.

'Wait,' Billy moaned, 'it might—'

'Shh,' said Mirabelle, and she scraped the nail along the clamp as hard as she could.

There was the screech of metal against metal, and Billy spasmed for a moment and then lay still.

Mirabelle dropped the nail. 'Billy?'

Billy threw a forearm across his eyes and winced. 'That hurt.'

'Good,' said Mirabelle.

Billy looked further wounded by the comment.

'Sorry,' said Mirabelle.

She helped him off the floor and then they both tore off their clamps and flung them away. Mirabelle looked at the door.

'I presume it's locked.'

'Doesn't matter,' said Billy, striding towards it. He started to pant gutturally, his eyes turned black, and Mirabelle watched, fascinated, as his hands became clawed.

He grabbed the handle, pressed his shoulder against the door, and pushed.

The door gave way, sending up a plume of splinters and sawdust. Billy and Mirabelle peeked out into the hallway.

It was narrow and grubby, with walls that hadn't seen a decent coat of paint in years. It smelt musty and old, and Billy wrinkled his nose as he sniffed the air.

'Where to now?' Mirabelle whispered.

'That way,' said Billy, pointing left. Mirabelle started to move, but Billy grabbed her arm and sniffed the air. 'Wait. There's someone down there.'

They crept along the hallway. It led to the top of a short flight of wooden stairs. Billy raised his hand and Mirabelle stopped. What seemed like an eternity passed, and Mirabelle could almost feel her heart hammering against her ribs. Billy pointed down the stairs to the right.

'Someone's definitely down there,' he whispered. 'Take it slow and follow my lead.'

They crept forward and, as they moved, Mirabelle was convinced that the sound of every step they made was magnified a thousand-fold. There were only a few stairs to go when a bulky bald man stepped out of a doorway below. They were above his eye level, and Mirabelle was just about to snag Billy's arm and whisper that they should retreat when the man looked up and saw them.

An 'Oi!' was all he managed before Billy leapt upon him, sending him flying against a wall.

'Run!' Billy shouted.

Mirabelle was frozen for a moment as she saw the man spring back up and hurl himself at Billy. He tried to grab him, but Billy ducked, grabbed one of his arms and pulled.

The man blanched a milky white and gave a high-pitched shriek before collapsing on to his knees.

Mirabelle ran down the last few steps just in time to see two more men run up the hallway from the back of the house.

'I said run! I'll hold them off!' Billy shouted. His teeth were long now, his eyes completely black and his vicious lupine smile made it look as if he were enjoying the prospect of what was to come.

Mirabelle bolted.

She found herself running into a yard filled with old bits of scrap metal and farm machinery. There were sheds and outhouses either side of her. The ground was wet and mucky after what must have been a rainstorm, and she found herself slipping as she hurtled forward. She managed to right herself just in time to stop plunging headfirst into the blades of an ancient rusted plough.

Mirabelle ran through the yard and found herself in an

outer courtyard bounded by a wall and a massive wooden gate. Unfortunately, the gate was padlocked. She rattled the lock in frustration before frantically looking left and right for another escape route.

There was what looked like an old barn to her left. She ran to it, looking for cover, hoping against hope that it might have a back door or an exit of some sort. She flinched when she saw a couple of ravens strutting outside the barn in search of food, but fortunately none of them was Thorne's pet.

The barn stank and it was so gloomy one would be forgiven for thinking it was night outside rather than daylight.

Mirabelle was panting hard now, and she ducked behind a ladder, looking for a means of escape at the rear of the barn.

There was nothing, just a slatted wall of mouldy-looking wooden planks. She pushed at it, hoping that it might be old and weak, but nothing gave. She punched it, kicked it.

She heard wing beats behind her, and an almost mocking 'caw'.

The pied raven had settled on a low ledge, its eyes sparkling with malice.

Mirabelle had had enough. There was a shovel leaning against the wall. She grabbed it and rushed the raven, swinging at it with all her might.

The raven shot upwards, cawing furiously as Mirabelle missed it by inches. It flapped above her, going higher and higher.

'You could do yourself an injury with that.'

Mirabelle turned to see Thorne leaning nonchalantly against the door jamb.

'Get out of my way,' she growled.

'Or what?' he said.

Mirabelle rushed him. Thorne grabbed the shaft of the shovel with ease and, as they both grappled with it, he grinned at her.

'You have some fight in you for a puny one.'

He pulled hard. Mirabelle felt as if her arms were being wrenched from her sockets. Thorne barely got a chance to throw the shovel aside before she let go and launched herself at him. She felt small and ridiculous, but she was angry. Angry because of everything this man had done, so she threw herself at him and pummelled him with her fists.

Thorne laughed, then lifted her off the ground. Mirabelle hit him in the face and she could see he was getting angry now too. Out of the corner of her eye she saw something flit past, and instinctively she reached out, bellowing for aid.

The two ravens she'd spotted outside flew into the barn in response to her summons. They both dived at Thorne's face, shrieking and pecking. Thorne refused to let Mirabelle go, and her hand closed round something on his chest as she tried to push herself away. She lashed out with a punch, hitting him in the eye. He instantly dropped her, and the thing she'd gripped came away in her hands. Mirabelle took advantage of the fact that he was doubled over clutching his eye and ran out out into the courtyard.

The ravens followed. She let them go and they soared up into the sky.

She was still holding the object she'd ripped from Thorne. Looking at it stopped her in her tracks.

It was a stone pendant that had been held in place by nothing more than some old, frayed string. She recognised the symbols instantly.

A sun and moon separated by a sword.

She turned to see Thorne standing in the doorway of the barn, unable to cross the threshold because of the sun that blazed in the sky.

Billy

Billy had made his way to the roof of the house as two of the men scrambled after him, while their bald companion stumbled around below groaning and nursing his arm. His pursuers roared at him as he effortlessly pivoted round a cornice and found himself facing a tall boundary wall. He looked at the wall and back to the two men, who were dragging a ladder between them from the side of the house.

Billy thought about waiting. That way he would be ready when the ladder was in place, then it would just be a matter of a well-timed push and both men would go crashing back to earth.

But the wall wasn't far away, at least not for him. He could make the jump easily. They couldn't.

Billy leapt from the roof and landed on top of the wall, but the wall was old and his right foot landed on a crumbly brick. His leg went from under him, his left knee hit the wall as he tumbled over the edge and he bit down on his tongue, gasping at the pain.

He'd fallen further than this before, but he was taken by surprise. He spent a few moments on his back, blinking up into the canopy of trees, listening to the birdsong, which seemed so incongruous to him now. He heard the warbling of a thrush and the faraway squawks of jackdaws.

Billy sat up and rubbed his knee. It was slightly numb, but he knew it would be all right soon enough. Behind the wall, he heard his two pursuers grumbling angrily.

He stood up and hopped along by the boundary wall for a few moments, then started to pick up speed. He sniffed the air, found what he was looking for and headed in its direction.

He came upon a large wooden gate. He knew Mirabelle was behind it. He could hear her talking. There was a hole in one of the planks and he looked through it.

He could just about see Mirabelle. She was standing in a courtyard, and there was something dangling from one of her hands. She held it up and shook it angrily.

The wind shifted slightly and Billy's hackles raised as he caught a whiff of Thorne's scent. He was clearly just out of view, and Billy could hear Mirabelle shouting, 'Tell me!'

Billy's two pursuers huffed and puffed into the scene, and Billy had to fight the urge to shout a warning to Mirabelle. Both men went to grab her, but Billy was delighted to see Mirabelle shrug them off, barely acknowledging them in her anger. She stepped out of view and the two men followed. Billy heard her shouting again, and then she reappeared, being dragged between them.

Billy watched as they headed in the direction of the house, then flinched as Thorne appeared in his eyeline, a lot closer to the gate than he'd expected.

Billy lay flat against the gate for a few moments, holding his breath. He gave it a few moments then looked again.

Thorne was looking at the gate while fixing something round his neck. He seemed different to Billy somehow. There was still that sullen fury coming off him in waves, but there was something else too, something new in his eyes.

The pied raven swooped into view and landed on his shoulder. Thorne turned and walked away.

Billy relaxed and sat down for moment.

Yes, there had definitely been something new in Thorne's demeanour. Something that gave Billy hope.

Billy smiled, because he knew fear when he saw it.

Piglet

A train station.

That's what they call it, thinks Piglet.

All hustle and bustle. Bustle and hustle. People moving this way and that, breathless, hurried. The train sits there, huffing and chuffing in its great cloud of steam like a benevolent iron dragon. All heat and iron pulsing in preparation for the off.

Piglet stands on the platform in the midst of it all. He remembers a story Mirabelle read to him once about a train station.

And Dr Ellenby had been on a train more than once.

In fact, Dr Ellenby had gone on a train on a sunny day to Cornwall to see someone . . .

The memory was soft and filled with light and happiness. Dr Ellenby's memory. Dr Ellenby on a train. And Piglet caught Dr Ellenby's reflection in the window, and he was younger, much younger. His face was shaven and he was smiling, and he was thinking about . . .

Rebecca.

Yes. Lovely. A white cotton dress billowing in a summer breeze. The sea glittering. Blue like her eyes. That feeling in his chest. Proud. Happy. Like he could fly. Oh, how he could fly. He could soar. When she smiled . . .

Piglet shakes his head. The memory melts away.

'Concentrate, Piglet.'

He remembers Mirabelle's words.

Piglet nods. He will concentrate.

A woman rushes past, dragging a suitcase with one hand and a small child with the other. A man in a brown suit frowns and scrutinises his watch before clambering up into the train. An old couple link arms as they hobble along the platform and the steam swallows them up. A couple and their four children hurry along while a porter leans out of the train and shouts something. One of the four children is a small boy with a lollipop. He turns. Sees Piglet. Stops.

So many more people now, flowing around him like a river. The boy is still looking at him. He smiles at Piglet. Then he waves.

So many people.

Piglet observes them. He can feel the old familiar tickle of curiosity.

Just a quick look. It wouldn't hurt, would it? Just to take a quick look.

Piglet closes his eyes. Piglet dissipates. No one is watching him, so it's easy. He is a small speck among the sea of people, and now he is even more invisible, and he floats above them, looks at them, smiles.

And down he swoops.

And he sees and hears everything.

'. . . we'll be late we'll be late . . .'

The woman herding her four children is panicky, edgy. Her husband is thinking about old cricket scores.

. . . fifteen centuries . . . Philpott . . . two more and he would have . . .

The porter thinking about his tea . . .

. . . sausage, bacon, eggs, lovely dripping . . .

All their thoughts a swirl and a dance as Piglet moves between them, one to the other to each to everyone, and they are thinking about hats and tea and shopping and dresses and football and mud and rain in a dark blue night the way it moves steam lollipop lollipop I like lollipops the boy is funny small and large and he was in the air the magic boy made of lights.

And Piglet is almost lost in the glory of it, like swimming in a roaring river on a bright blue sunny day with the world thundering in his ears.

'Concentrate, Piglet!'

Piglet stops. He has to remember what he's here for. What he's promised himself to do.

Piglet moves on the air up and away from the people and towards the train. He materialises on a seat in one of the train carriages. He looks out of the window.

The boy with the lollipop is on the platform looking right at him. He waves at Piglet again. This time Piglet waves back.

Piglet turns away and settles in his seat. He doesn't see the man on the platform blink and stumble and hold his chest, doesn't see the sudden panic on his face. He doesn't see the man's wife react in much the same way, doesn't see how she looks at her husband and the other people in horror. That look of recognition they now share because they've just shared everything, and they know each other. Someone screams, but Piglet doesn't hear it. Then the babbling starts, the strange anxiety-ridden recriminations, the shouting of several voices at once.

It takes quite a while for all the commotion to finally calm down, but somehow it does. People fix their hats, check their suitcases, they avoid each other's eyes. And they all make a silent agreement to pretend nothing ever happened.

Eventually, they start to pile on to the train, but no one takes a seat near Piglet. People are nervous, skittish, every one of them seems keen to pretend that nothing has happened on the platform, but some of them are still whispering among *themselves, and they look frightened.*

A whistle pierces the air. There is a grinding sound, Piglet is pushed gently forward and then back as the train begins to move. Huff chuff huff chuff, getting louder and faster. Huffchuff huff. Huffchuff huff.

Piglet looks at the empty seat across from him, and frowns now because his eyes feel strange. For a moment he was thinking about Dr Ellenby again. On a train. On his way to Cornwall, many years ago.

The small boy and his family tumble past him down the aisle in a flurry of suitcases and limbs as they try to find a seat, and Piglet can hear the small boy with his lollipop ask his mother:

'Why is the magic boy crying?'

Mirabelle

It was dark outside, and the room was cold. Mirabelle sat under the boarded-up window with her knees pulled up. The fury she'd felt since confronting Thorne had not left her. If anything, it was getting worse with each passing moment. Seeing the pendant had somehow made her more angry. She supposed because it was another deception. Yet another in a long line of them, stretching back to Billy and maybe even further. Her thoughts were wild and angry. She thought about Enoch the day she'd confronted him about her mother. It was a buried enmity that bubbled back to the surface now. She had forgiven him, hadn't she? Maybe she hadn't, because the anger she felt was real now, and she thought about Odd and the others, the secrets they'd all kept.

She felt panicked in her anger, like someone set adrift. She slapped the heel of her hand against the wooden floor in an effort to distract herself from her thoughts.

The door opened. Thorne stepped in, glowering. Mirabelle glowered back at him, rubbing her sore hand. He opened his sneering mouth, but Mirabelle refused to let him get a word out.

'Which house?' she demanded.

Thorne wrinkled his nose. 'What?'

'Come on, which house are you from? Which sanctuary? Certainly not Rookhaven – I'd know that. House Pemberton maybe? Or Annsley Manor? Not Montforth anyway, or Heskton. Too grand for the likes of you.' She jutted her chin out defiantly. 'You're not human, you're Family, but for some reason you're pretending to be human. Why is that?'

'You shut your mouth now,' Thorne snarled.

'Or what? You'll set your little raven on me? You're not the only one who can do that, you know. I can do it too. And I can do it again, just like that.' She snapped her fingers.

For some reason, Thorne looked momentarily rattled, but all the while he was studying her face. Mirabelle turned away from him.

'You'll do what you're told from here on in. You'll behave,' he said.

'Why'd you come in here?'

'You'll behave,' he said, pointing at her.

'Do you work for the man that Billy spoke of? Is that what you do?'

Thorne took a step towards her. 'I hunt,' he said, a wild look in his eyes. 'It's what I'm good at. I set traps. I make devices. I hunt.'

'You hunt your own kind? For money? Or are you like some kind of dim-witted hunting dog that can be ordered around?'

Thorne bellowed with rage, grabbed the chair, and flung it against the wall. One leg splintered, and the chair bounced back off the wall and landed on the floor. He was panting now, his eyes red-rimmed, nostrils flaring as he loomed over Mirabelle. And yet Mirabelle felt a strange calm because she'd caught a flicker of fear beneath all that rage. And then there was the panicked way he kept studying her face, as if he were looking for something.

'Misbegotten!'

He almost spat the word out. Mirabelle felt the embers of her anger flare again.

'Misbegotten and proud,' she said, rising to her feet.

'Pah!' said Thorne, running a hand through his stringy hair and turning away from her in contempt.

'Proud of my mother. Proud of who she was even though I barely knew her. Proud of Alice of Rookhaven!' Mirabelle felt strong and suffused with righteous anger. She'd never referred to her mother that way before, never thought to give her a title, but it seemed right somehow.

Thorne didn't move. It looked as if he were frozen to the spot.

'Alice?' he said.

'Yes,' said Mirabelle, suddenly feeling very unsure of herself. She didn't like the tone in his voice. It was softer.

Thorne was still turned away from her. One hand on his head. 'Ravens. You can summon ravens.'

Mirabelle's mouth felt dry. 'Yes,' she croaked.

Thorne said something then, but Mirabelle wasn't sure

what she'd just heard. She could feel a roaring in her ears, and her vision seemed blurred.

'What did you say?' she said. The roaring was getting louder, but somehow she heard the words now as Thorne turned back towards her.

'I said, you have your mother's eyes.'

Mirabelle rocked back on her feet as if she'd been struck a physical blow.

'How could you have known my mother?'

Thorne's face was a tumult of emotions now. Fear, anger, shock, sorrow.

'Where is she now?' he asked. 'Is she safe? Tell me she's safe,' he said, advancing on her.

Mirabelle took a step back, shaking her head.

'She died, when she gave birth to me, she . . .'

Thorne's face contorted. He seemed to be in agony as he looked wildly around the room. This was something Mirabelle recognised only too well. This was grief. Her heart began to pound as she began to piece the puzzle together.

'Mirabelle,' said Thorne, his voice hoarse. 'I remember now. I remember Alice saying she liked that name . . .'

Mirabelle looked at the floor. She was trembling all over. She shook her head violently.

'You're not . . . you're not . . . no . . .'

Thorne stumbled towards her, his hand held out.

There was no way this man was her father.

'Get out!' Mirabelle screamed at him. 'Get out!'

Thorne blinked in shock.

'Get away from me!'

Thorne looked stricken. Eventually, he turned and left the room.

Mirabelle stood looking at the door, her nails biting into her palms.

Billy

As time passed, it was becoming clearer to Billy that he was torn between two courses of action.

Choice one was to get his bearings and head to London alone to try to rescue Meg. Thinking about it inflamed him, set his thoughts a jumble and turned him into a quivering ball of anger.

Yes, rescue Meg.

But how?

And that was where he stumbled. As soon as brute logic took hold, he knew there was no guarantee he could get her back. Then there was the second problem. He could leave here and try to rescue Meg, but that would mean leaving Mirabelle. Billy felt trapped between rage on one hand and guilt on the other. Meg was family, but wasn't Mirabelle family of sorts too, and hadn't he betrayed her? Surely he owed her something?

He stood outside the boundary wall, flexing his fingers. Then he made his decision.

Mirabelle

Mirabelle felt an odd mixture of relief and despair when the door opened and Billy was unceremoniously flung into the room. He stumbled and fell against the table.

'They found you.'

Billy grinned sheepishly while rubbing his arm. 'Nah, I gave myself up.'

'What?'

Billy came and sat beside her. 'Gave myself up.' He shrugged.

Mirabelle gaped at him. 'Why?'

Billy looked everywhere except at her. 'I couldn't just leave you here, not after everything I did.' He looked awkward and embarrassed.

'Besides, they're going to take us to where they're keeping Meg.'

'You could have gone by yourself. You could have tried to save her.'

Billy shook his head. 'Wouldn't have worked. Anyway, I couldn't leave you.'

Mirabelle felt a warm glow. She smiled at Billy, but once again he studiously avoided her gaze.

'You are, you know,' she said.

He gave her a suspicious look. 'What?'

'Forgiven.'

He nodded in gratitude. Both of them sat in silence for a moment.

'Sort of,' said Mirabelle.

She smiled at him again and he smiled shyly back, but she could still see the guilt in his eyes.

'We'll get her back together, I promise,' said Mirabelle.

'I know,' said Billy.

The door opened an hour later. The two men who had dragged Mirabelle here stepped in and ordered Billy and Mirabelle to follow them downstairs. The four of them stepped out into the light to find Thorne standing in front of the house beside a van. The raven was on his shoulder. The men escorted Mirabelle and Billy to the back of the van, then one of them threw open the doors and growled, 'Get in.'

Mirabelle ignored him and turned to look at Thorne. 'You're going to keep working for your paymaster, even knowing what you know now?'

Thorne couldn't look at her. He shook his head. 'It changes nothing.'

Mirabelle stepped closer to him. 'It changes everything.'

Mirabelle sensed the strange unease that rippled through Thorne's men as they watched this exchange, and she could feel Billy's eyes on her.

'I have a job to finish,' Thorne replied.

'And what exactly *is* that job?'

'You'll find out when we get there,' said Thorne. He gestured for her to get into the van and the dismissive way he did it infuriated Mirabelle, but she did as she was told and stepped up into the oil-stinking windowless interior. Billy sat on a bench riveted to the wall, but Mirabelle stood and looked at Thorne insolently.

'You haven't answered my question.'

Thorne held the door and sighed, then finally looked Mirabelle straight in the eye.

'We're going to see how well you take after your father. You're going to help me lay a trap.'

With that he slammed the doors shut.

Piglet

Piglet has never seen so many people.

The world is alive with noise and light and the motion of crowds. He has stepped off the train into the vastness of the station and is immediately engulfed by wave upon wave of scurrying people. The click clack of high heels, the tramp of boots, men in great big tweed overcoats wearing homburgs, women in long rain macs, boys in shorts and shirts and girls with ringlety hair, the squalling of babies in prams, an old one-legged man in a long military coat trying to sell matches while leaning against a pillar, line upon line of people crossing and criss-crossing, the sounds of their feet and the constant murmur echoing up into the ceiling.

For a moment, Piglet doesn't know what to do.

He blinks at the majesty of it all. All those thoughts and dreams compacted into one place. And outside, just a step away through an arch – London.

He understands these words now, knows what they mean to these people, how the slow words fix them in place so they can direct themselves through their small yet multifarious lives.

London.

Home.

Streets.

And names too. Names fix things in place. Names like . . .

Mirabelle.

Marcus.

Odd.

Piglet shakes himself. He is getting distracted. He remembers that he has something to do. He walks on through the station, instinctively avoiding the rushing passers-by, his eyes fixed on one prize. He steps out into the light of a city teeming with life, walks past shopfronts and houses, through streets he knows thanks to Billy, names of places he recognises thanks to Billy.

And thanks to Billy only one word is uppermost in his mind right now.

He holds fast to it.

Meg.

Part 6
The Vulsifier

Mirabelle

'We're in London,' said Billy.

'How can you tell?' asked Mirabelle.

'I can smell it,' he said.

The van lurched to the side, and Mirabelle was thrown from her bench. Billy grabbed her arm and helped her back into a sitting position as he wobbled back and forth in an effort to keep his balance. Mirabelle noticed how he couldn't seem to look her in the eye again, but it was different this time, as if now he was afraid to broach something for fear of offending her.

He sat back down, wringing his hands.

'What is it?' asked Mirabelle.

'Nothing,' said Billy.

'There's something on your mind,' said Mirabelle.

Billy seemed to be attempting to screw up his courage. 'That thing Thorne said to you about your father – what did he mean?'

Now it was Mirabelle's turn to look away. 'I'd rather not talk about it.'

'It's just . . . it sounded . . .'

Mirabelle shook her head.

Billy nodded and didn't press the matter.

The van stopped moments later. Billy stood up first,

wiping his mouth, staring at the back doors. Mirabelle waved at him to relax.

The doors opened, and Thorne stood there with Abelard on his shoulder.

'Out.'

Mirabelle and Billy climbed down and found themselves within an enclosed cobbled courtyard ringed by the architecture of a large gothic house. The walls loomed above them, hemming them in, adding to a terrible sense of suffocation.

Thorne muttered something to his two henchmen, they nodded and both climbed back into the van. Thorne clicked his fingers and pointed at a spot in front of him.

'Where I can see you,' he said.

Mirabelle and Billy stepped in front of him. Mirabelle tried to catch his eye, but Thorne couldn't bring himself to look at her.

He pointed in front of them. 'Through that door.'

'Why?' said Billy.

'You want to see your sister, don't you?' Thorne snapped.

'Of course he does,' said Mirabelle. 'Just as any normal person would want to be with their family.'

She could see Thorne's jaw muscle tighten. 'Just get inside,' he hissed.

They stepped through the oak-panelled double doors and into a long hallway, its walls a faded lemon colour. Dark and austere-looking portraits of nobility lined the walls.

'We could run,' said Mirabelle, feeling the sudden urge to annoy him.

'You won't,' said Thorne, brushing past her.

Both Mirabelle and Billy looked at each other.

'Come on,' barked Thorne, his voice ringing off the walls and ceiling.

They followed him down the hallway.

He took a sharp right at the end of the hall, then pushed through a pair of heavy double doors. They followed him into a small library. Its shelves were of black wood, its floors and ceilings grey. It was lit by bulbs from several green sconces along the walls. There were two tall windows stretching from floor to ceiling opposite the door. Both had iron bars over them. There was a long oak table, and six leather chairs around it.

'Wait here,' said Thorne.

He turned to leave but hesitated.

'Afterwards, when all this is done, we can talk,' he said to Mirabelle.

'I don't know if I want to talk to you,' she replied.

Thorne looked at a loss. 'We can go somewhere private.'

'I'm not going anywhere without Piglet. I don't go anywhere without my family. Unlike some people I could name.'

Thorne looked furious. 'Just wait here,' he spat.

'Aren't you going to use your magic clamps this time?' taunted Mirabelle.

'You both have reasons to stay,' said Thorne.

'What's my reason?' said Mirabelle.

Thorne looked at her, then nodded at Abelard. 'Watch them,' he said.

Abelard flew up on to a shelf and hunched there, the light shining in his eyes.

Thorne swept out of the room, slamming the double doors behind him.

'What was all that about?' asked a perplexed Billy.

'Nothing,' said Mirabelle, pretending to be more interested in their new surroundings. She could still see Thorne's face. She was repulsed by it, but only because of what he'd done. Part of her was fascinated also, and she'd found herself examining his features for a family resemblance even as they'd argued. A resemblance she didn't want to find.

Billy went to the windows and immediately started to test the bars.

'There's no getting through these,' he said.

Abelard gave a low purring sound deep in the back of his throat as if mocking him.

Billy turned away from the window and started to look at the contents of the room, but Mirabelle knew when someone was feigning interest to hide the fact that something else was on their mind. She reckoned he was only playing for time and that he wanted to ask again about what Thorne had meant. She decided to distract him with a question of her own.

'Do you think Meg is here?'

'Yes. I remember this house.'

'And they promised they'd reunite you as soon as you brought Piglet to them?'

Billy nodded.

'And you believed them?'

Mirabelle couldn't help the tone of accusation that came into her voice. She felt slightly guilty when she saw the hurt and panic on Billy's face. She was about to say something, but the door opened and two new men walked in, followed by Thorne.

One of the men was a spindly-looking fellow with half-moon spectacles, wearing a white coat. The other was a well-dressed middle-aged man who walked with the aid of a cane.

Thorne pulled a seat across for the man. He sat down and placed his hands on the pommel of his cane, rested his chin on them, and smiled.

'Hello again, Billy,' he said. He turned his attention to Mirabelle. 'I'm Robert Courtney. And you are?'

Mirabelle took a step closer to him to show she wasn't afraid. 'Mirabelle. Mirabelle of Rookhaven. Daughter of Alice of Rookhaven.'

She shot a look at Thorne, who studiously avoided her gaze.

'She doesn't appear too fond of you, Mr Thorne. Why is that, I wonder?' said the man in the white coat.

Thorne clenched a fist and glared at a point on the floor.

Courtney pointed his cane at the man with half-moon

spectacles. 'This is Professor Aspinall. He is a man at the forefront of a new science, one he likes to call metaphysical mechanics. He studies the soul, the spirit, life itself.'

Mirabelle stared at the professor. She didn't like him. He had a dangerous, almost hungry, look in his eyes.

'You are from Rookhaven, girl?' he said.

Mirabelle nodded. 'My name is Mirabelle. It was a name given to me by my mother.'

Aspinall smirked. 'Really, and did your father have no say in the matter?'

Mirabelle couldn't help herself. Her eyes flicked to Thorne, who averted his gaze from her. Mirabelle tried to hide the gesture by looking around the room, but the damage had been done.

Aspinall put a hand to his mouth and laughed, looking from Mirabelle to Thorne and back again. 'Oh my! *Oh my!*'

Courtney frowned and looked at him. 'What is it?'

'You said she was Misbegotten: half human, half Family,' said Aspinall, ignoring Courtney while grinning at Thorne. 'I'd heard rumours about you, Mr Thorne, and it seems they may have been true.'

Thorne just looked at the floor. Mirabelle almost felt sorry for him. She could feel a prickling on her scalp as she saw him clench both hands.

'You didn't tell me she was yours,' Aspinall said gleefully.

Mirabelle heard Billy give a great intake of breath. He looked at her, as if searching her face for an explanation. Mirabelle couldn't speak.

Aspinall started guffawing, then reached into his inside pocket. 'This is an important discovery. I shall take notes. I could get an academic paper out of—'

Thorne grabbed Aspinall, lifted him straight off his feet and pushed him against a wall, jamming a forearm into the scientist's neck. Aspinall started choking, writhing like an eel stabbed with a fork.

'Mr Thorne,' admonished Courtney.

Thorne pushed Aspinall harder. The man's face turned red. Mirabelle was surprised to find herself almost urging Thorne on.

'Mr Thorne! Enough!' Courtney roared.

Thorne slowly let the professor go. Aspinall collapsed to his knees, gasping and clutching at his neck, yet amazingly he still found it within himself to laugh.

'Quite . . . quite amazing . . .'

He staggered to his feet and ran a hand through his hair while looking at Thorne. Thorne glared back, nostrils flaring. Mirabelle could see that he was trembling.

'Is it true, Mr Thorne?' asked Courtney.

'Is what true?' said Thorne, his eyes still fixed on Aspinall.

Courtney pointed at Mirabelle with his cane. 'Is this girl your daughter?'

Thorne still refused to look at Mirabelle. 'I believe so,' he finally said.

Mirabelle felt suddenly light-headed. She could feel their eyes on her, saw the dumb-founded look on Billy's face.

Courtney looked perturbed. 'This presents a difficulty,' he said.

Aspinall made his way to him, one hand still pressed to his neck. 'In what way?'

Courtney looked shifty. 'In a moral sense.'

Aspinall spluttered. 'Moral? Ha!'

'We need to consider our intentions, professor.'

Aspinall bent down towards him and made a fist. 'We know what we want to do. We have a use for her. We can use her to bring the creature to us. She has a connection with it. I've heard stories about this one. She's the one who defeated the Malice.' He stood up and looked at Thorne. 'Unless her dear father objects to her being used.'

Thorne stood sideways, slouched forward like a gorilla, still refusing to take part in the conversation.

'We can let her go afterwards,' said Courtney, rotating his cane this way and that between the palms of his hands. 'She will be of no use to us once we have the creature.'

'And the boy?' said Courtney.

Aspinall shrugged. 'He can go too. When all this is done.'

'When all of *what* is done?' Mirabelle growled.

Both men looked at her. Courtney was about to speak when Billy decided to intercede.

'Where's my sister? I want her back right now,' he said.

'You sister is safe,' said Courtney, playing fretfully with his cane as if his mind were elsewhere. 'You'll be reunited with her when the task is accomplished.'

'And then we can leave?' said Billy.

Courtney nodded agitatedly. Mirabelle looked at him closely. He was chewing on his lip now and rubbing his chin. She caught Aspinall looking at her and smiling to himself as if considering a private joke.

'As a scientist, I'm rather curious about something,' Aspinall said at last. 'I like to observe things, tease matters out. Find the correlation between cause and effect.' He almost bowed to Courtney. 'If you would permit me, sir, I'd like to tell the girl a little tale.'

Courtney gave him a nod. 'Be quick.'

Aspinall straightened up and smiled.

'Once there was a creature . . . His name isn't important, but suffice to say he was a member of a race of beings calling themselves the Family.'

Abelard gave a caw and fluttered his wings. Mirabelle glanced at Thorne, who was looking at the floor.

'Now this creature had remarkable skills. He was strong, agile, cunning, and he had a facility for what some might call magic. He had an extraordinary ability to track others, create strange devices and do it all with stealth.

'The so-called *Family* didn't care much for these talents, and the creature was content to tinker away in his own fashion. In the meantime, the Family came to an understanding with members of the human race. They drew up an agreement known as the Covenant. This agreement meant neither side could do harm to the other.'

Aspinall shook his head and chuckled as he looked at

Mirabelle. She wrinkled her nose in disgust at him.

'However, both sides reckoned without the occasionally ungovernable nature of the other: a monstrous nature that could not be thwarted.'

'Monsters,' said Mirabelle. 'That's what you like to call us, but we're more than that.'

'Where is this leading, Professor?' said a clearly irritated Courtney.

'You see, there were those in the Family who could not put aside their instincts. These members preferred to continue to hunt humans in the outside world. And since they were breaking this new sacred trust, they were considered outcasts. You know the types of creature I'm talking about, don't you, boy?'

Aspinall smirked at Billy. Billy looked defiantly back at him. 'The Catchpoles didn't deserve what you did to them.'

Aspinall shrugged. 'They were outcasts, the lowest of the low, scrabbling for meat like beasts. They deserved nothing.'

Billy was quivering now. He looked ready to pounce, but Mirabelle placed a gentle hand on his arm and shook her head.

'It was decided that creatures who broke the Covenant and feasted upon humans needed to be hunted down. But every hunt needs a hunter, and this is where this particular creature and his talents came in. One whose skills could finally be put to good use.'

Aspinall looked at Thorne now. 'How accurate have I

been so far, Mr Thorne? Is there anything you would like to add to *your* story?'

Thorne clenched his jaw and worked his thumbs against his knuckles. Mirabelle almost pitied him.

'With regard to how you meted out justice, we won't pry, Mr Thorne. For me it's enough to know what your status was in this underground society of yours. You were the one who hunted your own kind. The one they were too ashamed to even acknowledge.'

There was notable disgust in the way Aspinall spoke to Thorne. Mirabelle felt a quick pulse of rage.

'I did my duty! I just did what was asked of me!' Thorne shouted.

'And what *was* asked of you, Mr Thorne? What did this *duty* involve? How did your beloved family repay you?' asked Aspinall mildly.

Thorne looked unsure of himself, maybe even slightly ashamed. Aspinall looked from him to Mirabelle and back again.

'Oh, I see,' said Aspinall. 'You'd rather your daughter didn't know that you were shunned by your own kind.'

Courtney rolled his eyes and sighed. 'Are you finished?'

'Almost,' said Aspinall. He licked his lips. 'Mr Thorne dealt with outcasts. This involved moving in the human world. It was there he met a woman called Alice. Now Mr Thorne knew there had been some history of Family members consorting with humans. Sometimes they even had children together.' Aspinall shook his head ruefully. 'However, these children became known as the Misbegotten. They were treated with even more revulsion than those who hunted humans in contravention of the Covenant. These children became outcasts among outcasts.'

Aspinall looked at Mirabelle and Billy now and sighed theatrically. 'One could almost feel sorry for them.'

No one said anything for a moment until Mirabelle took a step forward. 'Perhaps you could tell me about my mother, since you seem to know so much.'

The look Aspinall gave her was smug and condescending. 'Ah, but there is only one person who can tell you about *that* side of the story, so unfortunately this is where my expertise ends.'

Mirabelle looked at her father. It was still too strange for her to consider him as such. The word *father* just seemed alien and wrong. She didn't know how she could be related to someone who disgusted her so much. Thorne refused to look at her.

'My mother was alone when she came to look for sanctuary in Rookhaven. Why was that? Where were you?' she asked him. Thorne just shook his head.

There was a sharp rapping sound as Courtney banged his cane on the floor.

'Enough! We have a project to complete.'

'Yes, sir,' said Aspinall.

Mirabelle glared at the two men. Now more than ever she wished the ravens were with her.

Aspinall looked over his shoulder at Thorne. 'We have

the master of traps and contrivances here, and we have his daughter, who we can use as bait. Isn't that wonderfully ironic?'

Billy suddenly started laughing. He was laughing so hard he had to wipe tears from his eyes. Even Mirabelle and Thorne were taken by surprise by his outburst.

'You find something amusing?' asked Courtney.

Billy stopped laughing and shook his head in disbelief. 'There won't be any need for bait,' he said.

'Why is that?' asked a perplexed Aspinall.

Something about the way Billy smiled at him made Mirabelle's heart leap.

Billy

The feeling had come to Billy halfway through Aspinall's speech about Thorne. It was a curious mixture of dread and joy. He had the sudden inexplicable sense that something was coming, and then there were flashes of images again, images and feelings he'd forgotten.

Meg's face. Mirabelle's face.

He'd had to steady himself, and no one else in the room had noticed. His thoughts kept returning to his confrontation with Piglet.

No, not confrontation. The word *melding* seemed more appropriate. Yes, his melding with Piglet back in the town. They'd shared memories, thoughts, feelings.

He saw Meg's tear-stained face again, and Mirabelle's. Felt the imminent approach of something like a tidal wave . . . Something powerful and wild.

And now he understood.

Aspinall was advancing towards him, but something in the way Billy looked at him stopped the scientist in his tracks. Courtney had half risen from his chair. Thorne was frowning at him. Even Mirabelle seemed to detect a sudden shift in the atmosphere.

Billy felt the change in the air. The strange subtle vibrations that meant only one thing. In the distance he heard someone scream in terror.

He turned to Mirabelle and smiled.

'Piglet's here,' he said.

Piglet

Piglet looks at the house.

He can sense the movement within, things wafting on the air, familiar scents and sounds and heartbeats.

He can sense Mirabelle and he almost bursts with joy.

He walks towards the dark, forbidding door. A man steps towards him, glowering, gluttonous-looking, thuggish. He reaches to grab Piglet.

Piglet dissipates and passes through him, and as he does so he catches a glimpse of a grim, grey hovel, someone shouting, a dog snarling in a corner, a boy crying. Rain. A cracked window, spider-webbed and dirty.

Piglet enters the house.

The man is still screaming outside. Piglet pays him no more heed than an elephant would a gnat. He sniffs. He knows exactly where he has to go. He glides along a hallway, turns a corner.

The door he faces is grubby and yellow. Piglet condenses, becomes solid as rock, clawed and huge. He takes hold of the door handle. He turns it and rips it away. He drops the handle. The door swings open.

Piglet is careful now to reconstitute himself into the form of the boy.

He steps into the room.

It is gloomy and bare, but something stirs in the corner. Something small and ragged.

Piglet walks towards it.

He sees a shock of dirty blonde hair. Two bright blue eyes.

Meg looks up at him.

Piglet smiles at her.

Meg stands up and Piglet nods at her. She comes to him, takes his hand and smiles back.

They both go out into the hallway, hand in hand.

Piglet feels a strange calm now. He remembers when he first saw Billy's thoughts, the imagined capture of Meg, the searing almost physical absence of her, how much it had hurt and how Billy felt responsible for her.

And the fury he felt.

Piglet felt that fury too. He knew what it was to have someone close to you threatened. He imagined Mirabelle being taken from him; he could almost feel that same pain. He remembers a time when that seemed a frightening possibility. A time when the House of Rookhaven was threatened by something terrible. A time when he helped make something right. He wanted to make something right again. He wanted to make that decision himself.

And now, as he looks upon Meg, he feels his purpose is almost complete.

Except . . .

There is one more thing.

There is something else that Piglet feels he needs to know. Something missing, like part of a puzzle.

Images flicker through his mind as he walks with Meg. Images of Billy, of the Catchpoles, of a man in a white coat and a man with a cane. A terrible machine humming with dread power. Green mist blackening. Shards of glass.

Piglet feels something else. Something tugging at the very heart of him that tells him his mission isn't finished.

There is a door to his right. Black. Polished.

Piglet is curious. Piglet is always curious, and the sight of this door and the subtle vibrations that emanate from behind it make him more curious than ever.

Piglet opens the door. He steps into the room with Meg.

He sees what's in the room. Feels Meg squeeze his hand.

And now Piglet understands everything.

Mirabelle

Mirabelle's throat tightened when she saw Thorne reach into his long coat and take out an orb that looked exactly like the one Billy had used to capture Piglet. He flung the door open and ran from the room, his long coat and hair streaming behind him.

Mirabelle turned and chased after him without hesitation, evading the sweeping arc of Courtney's cane. There was a flash of white as Aspinall leapt towards her, fingers like claws as he reached for her. Mirabelle was grateful for the fact that Billy was there to push him aside. She heard Aspinall yelp in shock but didn't turn round. Piglet was her priority now.

She was aware of the commotion and shouting behind, but she and Billy ignored it as they pelted after Thorne.

They both rounded a corner to find Thorne halfway along a hallway, standing some distance away from two figures. One was a little girl.

The other was Piglet.

'Meg!' Billy shouted, and he started to run towards the girl.

Mirabelle tried to call him back. She'd seen Thorne raise the orb. Aspinall barged past her, and she could hear the *tap tap* of Courtney's stick behind her.

The orb opened. Golden light spilled from it.

Mirabelle recognised it as the same mysterious light that had originally trapped Piglet within the first orb.

Billy launched himself at the device and grabbed it.

Mirabelle shouted a warning to him, but Billy wasn't in the mood to listen to anybody. The light burned more fiercely, like a thing alive which knew him to be an enemy.

Billy snarled as he seemed to wrestle with it. The light shrieked in protest as he slammed the orb shut.

Billy

Everything was muffled, but there was a distant ringing in Billy's ears.

He got up off the floor which was now littered with fragments of the shattered orb, fizzing and trembling with thwarted magic. He heard something like distant cries. He shook his head to clear it.

The world came roaring back in.

Mirabelle was propped against a wall, blinking her eyes. Billy called to her and he felt relieved when she gave him a weak nod to reassure him she was all right. A few feet behind her, Aspinall was helping Courtney to stand.

Meg!

Billy tried to see her, but there was a strange golden haze obscuring that end of the corridor.

He could see Thorne trying to raise himself into a standing position by using the nearest wall.

Billy was surprised to note that he looked utterly terrified.

The haze started to fade and Billy saw Meg standing safely a few feet away behind something huge that seemed to flicker and change. Relief flooded through him. Piglet had obviously protected her from the blast by transforming himself, and now he was changing into something else. Something man-shaped. Billy's eyes widened in astonishment as he became an exact replica of Thorne. There was something surreal in seeing Thorne shouting at himself. Then the image of Thorne melted away and Piglet became a woman. She was pale with dark hair.

'No!' Thorne roared.

The woman shimmered and Mirabelle gasped. *Mother.* The vision lasted only a moment because now Piglet had taken on the form of Mirabelle.

'What's he doing?' Mirabelle whispered, crawling up beside Billy.

Billy shook his head. He was too stunned to speak.

And Piglet became the boy again.

An eerie silence descended, then Billy finally snapped out of it and went to move towards Meg, but he felt Mirabelle grab his arm and hiss, 'No!'

Three burly-looking men were running into the corridor. Each of them had a handgun.

'You took your time!' Courtney shouted at them. 'Take them.'

Billy was about to leap when one of the men grabbed Meg, but Mirabelle pulled him back.

'No! They have guns, Billy.'

The men took up positions behind Piglet and raised their guns.

Piglet stepped towards Thorne. Immediately the men poised themselves to fire.

'No, Piglet!' shouted Mirabelle.

'Hold your fire, gentlemen,' Courtney commanded.

Piglet advanced towards Thorne, smiling, holding his arms out with his wrists together. Thorne looked confused.

'No, don't,' Mirabelle cried, realising what was happening.

But Billy could see that Piglet had already made up his mind.

'He's surrendering,' he said.

Mirabelle

The sky was greying, and rain starting to spit down, as Mirabelle trudged across the courtyard with her fellow captives.

She still couldn't believe what she'd seen: Piglet giving himself up. It made no sense to her. She thought he would put up a fight at least.

Billy and Meg walked beside her. Billy had his arm round Meg, and despite their desperate situation Mirabelle felt happy for both of them. They were all flanked by Courtney's guards, while Piglet walked up ahead, almost as if he were leading the way. They were followed by Thorne, Aspinall and Courtney. Abelard was perched on Thorne's left shoulder.

'They said they'd let us go,' Billy whispered to her.

Mirabelle felt a hot twinge of irritation. 'And you believed them?'

Billy looked a little guilty. 'After it's done Aspinall said we can leave.'

But that was what concerned Mirabelle most of all. *After* what *was done?*

Billy looked away, and Mirabelle sneaked a glance at him. She knew he was only trying to convince himself that it would all turn out for the best. She saw the way he held on to Meg, tight and fearful, unwilling to let her go. It made her feel guilty, once again, for judging him so harshly.

They were heading towards what looked like a long stone shed with boarded-up windows. It looked as if it might have stored vehicles in the past.

One of the guards opened the double doors, and they were ushered into a large space with whitewashed walls. The air smelt of dirt and damp, and in the centre of the building was what looked like a brass machine of some sort. Mirabelle could hear a low hum coming from it, and the back of her neck tingled. The machine was covered in various dials and had a panel of glass tubes stuck to it. It had an observation window built into the front, and something else about it caught her eye too. At various intervals there were what looked like symbols etched into its surface. She saw Piglet tilt his head in curiosity when he caught sight of it.

'What's that?' she asked Billy.

'That, my dear, is the Vulsifier,' said Aspinall, grinning at her. 'It's my life's work, and I have the deep pockets of Mr Courtney to thank for helping me bring my creation to life.'

'It sucks the life out of people,' Billy whispered to her. 'Turns them to dust. He used it on the Catchpoles. He used it to kill them.'

'You really are a little ignoramus, aren't you?' sneered Aspinall as Billy looked at him accusingly. 'The Vulsifier does so much more than that.'

They were all lined up in front of the machine. One of the guards fetched Courtney a chair. He winced as he sat down. To Mirabelle, he looked haggard. He was sweating slightly, but there was feverish hope burning in his eyes. A desperation she hadn't noticed before. Meanwhile, Thorne stood near him, his eyes on the machine, still seemingly refusing to acknowledge Mirabelle's presence, as if he were hoping to wish her away merely by ignoring her.

Aspinall stood in front of the machine with his hands on his hips, running his eyes over its gleaming metallic surfaces, like a proud father standing before his child. He turned to everyone else present and wagged his finger.

'This machine is the only one of its kind in existence. It extracts the very essence of life from its subjects,' he said, beaming with delight.

'Subjects? Essence of life? You mean it kills people,' said Mirabelle.

'Oh, my dear, we're not talking about *people* in the strictest sense of the word. This extracts what's required from *monsters*.'

'And why would you need the essence of life? What good would it do?'

Aspinall was warming to his topic now, chattering with excitement.

'Because it extracts the essence from beings who are eternal and converts it into a form that can be absorbed – conferring long life on whoever consumes it.'

Mirabelle looked at Courtney sitting in his chair now,

perched on the edge, his face a mixture of agitation and hope. She looked at the way he held himself, at the twisted leg, his pallor. She wondered what else ailed him, and finally she began to understand. She took a step towards him. A guard grabbed her by the shoulder, but she shook him off, and Courtney signalled to the guard that it was all right for her to approach him.

'You want to live longer, don't you? That's why you had him make this for you,' she said.

Courtney's face contorted in a look of agony.

'You'd take the lives of other people just to prolong your own?'

Courtney turned his face away from her and muttered. 'Forgive me, you don't understand . . .'

Mirabelle turned her fury on Thorne now. 'And you! You helped with this. You should be ashamed.'

Abelard cawed on his shoulder. Thorne blinked as if he'd been slapped.

Mirabelle turned back to Aspinall. 'So you want to use Piglet. Why?'

Aspinall rubbed his hands together. 'Your friend has an especially vital quality. His energy, his life force, is particularly potent.'

'How do you know?' asked Billy.

Aspinall seemed to be taken by surprise by the question. Mirabelle saw his mask slip, just for a moment.

'I am a scientist,' he said, standing tall. 'I study the very nature of reality.'

Mirabelle stepped towards the machine and one of the guards went to block her, but Aspinall waved him back.

'If you're a scientist,' Mirabelle said, pointing at the machine. 'Then what do you need the magic runes for?'

And, again, Mirabelle saw the same flicker of uncertainty in Aspinall's eyes.

'Enough of this nonsense,' said Courtney. 'We're running out of time.'

'Very good, sir,' said Aspinall, giving a bow that Mirabelle thought was a little too obsequious. There was something about this man that didn't sit right with her. The idea of a human scientist using magical runes just didn't make sense.

Piglet stepped forward, and Mirabelle reached for him instinctively, but one of the guards grabbed her by the arm. Mirabelle wriggled in his grasp.

'Piglet! No!'

Piglet turned and looked at her. He had a gentle, almost aloof, look about him, as if he knew something no one else did. But Mirabelle knew better. She remembered something that Enoch had once said to her, that despite his age Piglet was 'little more than a child'.

Aspinall nodded at one of the guards, who stepped forward and started to unwind the wheel on the door at the side of the machine. The door swung open. The man turned towards Piglet.

'Wait!' Aspinall snapped, and for a moment, just for a fleeting moment, Mirabelle felt a surge of hope. She willed Piglet to transform, to become something horned and winged, breathing fire. Something that would crush these men and put them in their place. She could already feel his delicious rage, her delight at the looks on their faces.

Aspinall was looking at Piglet with an expression that was almost hungry. 'That's it, that's it,' he said, as if he were coaxing a puppy across a threshold.

Mirabelle shook her head. 'Piglet?'

Piglet looked at her. He gave a slow, sad smile.

Then he walked into the machine.

Piglet

Piglet enters the machine.

He has decided that this will be easiest. To fight would be simply fruitless. He doesn't see the point of struggling. It would not end well for Mirabelle and the others. Besides, Piglet is curious. He wants to see what happens next.

Meg and Billy are together again. This makes him happy. The rage and despair that Billy experienced over Meg's imprisonment had become part of Piglet when Piglet's mind had joined with his. It had spurred him on, and Piglet knew that if he rescued her it would alleviate Billy's pain. It would make him happy, and Piglet had seen enough of Billy's life to know that he deserved some happiness.

The door clangs shut behind him. Piglet nods to himself. He is used to such sounds.

Outside the window he sees the man called Aspinall turn some dials. Mirabelle is fighting and struggling and crying as the guard grips her arms. A white-faced Billy holds on to Meg.

Aspinall throws a lever. There is a look on his face of fearful excitement.

The air inside the machine comes alive with colour and sound. Piglet can feel the tingling charge, the sense of separation of something . . .

He looks at Mirabelle. Sees her face. Tries to remember it

from another time . . .

   . . . a happier time . . .

   . . . can't remember . . .

   He hears a sound, feels the onrush of something cold and dark.

   Marcus?

   Is this what it was like? Is this . . .

   Piglet feels the separation accelerate. Feels the darkness embrace him.

   Separating from everything, from the air from the world from all that binds and Piglet remembers . . . remembers . . .

   . . .Marcus's face . . . Mirabelle's face . . . smiling . . .

   . . . the house . . . the room . . . the fading in the mist . . .

   . . . is this what . . . is this . . . when . . . is . . .

   . . . Piglet is . . .

   Piglet is afraid.

   . . . Piglet . . .

   is

Part 7
Endings

Mirabelle

Mirabelle fell to her knees with her hands over her eyes. She gulped in air, but she couldn't get the image of Piglet vanishing out of her mind. It felt as if part of her had been ripped away.

And now there was the agony-filled silence, broken only by the low *tick tick* from the machine, like an engine cooling down.

She kept her eyes on the floor, refusing to look up.

She listened to Aspinall's footsteps, the sound of something being turned, and a snicking sound as if something was being disconnected from the machine, followed by Aspinall's 'Ah' of satisfaction.

'At last,' he said.

Out of the corner of her eye, Mirabelle could see Courtney rising unsteadily from his chair. He limped towards Aspinall, and Mirabelle forced herself to look at the so-called scientist.

He was holding a long glass tube. The tube was filled with a golden liquid light that roiled gently behind the glass, throwing out splashes of reflected shimmering gold.

Piglet.

Mirabelle felt sick to her stomach. She glanced at Thorne for a moment, and the look of sorrow and regret in

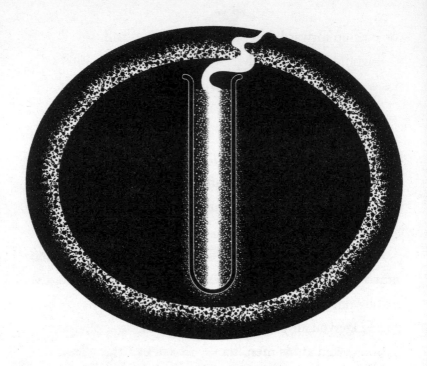

his eyes only made her more angry. Billy came to her and touched her arm.

'He's gone,' she sobbed. 'Piglet's gone.'

'Well, what do you think?' Aspinall said to Courtney.

'Beautiful. It looks absolutely beautiful.'

He was trembling, and there was that wretched hopeful look on his face again that Mirabelle now hated.

'Do you think it will work?' he asked, his voice cracking.

Aspinall nodded. 'Yes, I think it will.'

Courtney's eyes filled with tears. Aspinall patted him on the arm.

Then he kicked Courtney's cane out from under him and pushed him to the ground.

The move shocked Mirabelle and the others. Thorne

took a step forward, but Aspinall raised a hand.

'I wouldn't advise it, Mr Thorne. My men wouldn't take too kindly to any harm being done to my person.'

The three guards all raised their guns.

'*Your* men?' shouted Courtney, struggling to rise from the floor.

'That's right, Mr Courtney. Your wealth is rather inspiring, but I promised something more than you could ever give them.'

Aspinall was grinning at them all as he cradled the glass container to his chest. 'You've all been very useful, and I am quite grateful. To show my appreciation I think it's best that I give you all your just reward.'

He looked at his men, then pointed at Mirabelle.

'Stick them all in the machine, starting with this one.'

'No!'

All eyes turned to the source of the voice. Thorne was advancing on Aspinall with his fists clenched, eyes blazing.

Aspinall laughed. 'Oh, Mr Thorne, I see you've finally found your fatherly instincts. A little too late, don't you think?'

Aspinall gave a quick nod, and two of his men rushed to Thorne. Both raised the butts of their guns and struck him down. Abelard rose upwards, cawing and flapping in a fury as his master was pummelled. Thorne tried to cover his head, but the blows kept raining down, and just as it looked as if he might get to his feet another thug joined the fray.

'Stop it! Leave him alone!' Mirabelle shouted. She was

taken aback by the wave of panicked concern she suddenly felt. 'Call them off,' Mirabelle demanded.

Aspinall regarded her with disdain for a moment, then shouted: 'Enough. I think he's learned his lesson.'

The men backed away, leaving Thorne in a crumpled heap, his hands quivering above his head. Mirabelle had to fight the urge to go to him. He looked up for a moment and their eyes locked.

'You made me a promise,' croaked Courtney, now getting himself into a standing position. 'You said I could use the essence.'

Aspinall rolled his eyes. He started to speak, then his voice trailed off and he frowned.

Billy's grip on Mirabelle's arm tightened. She felt a sudden tingling, and the unmistakable tang of something metallic in the air.

A portal swirled open in the space between Mirabelle and Aspinall. Winthropp stepped through it, followed by his companion.

'Hello,' said Odd.

There was a moment, just a moment, when everything seemed to freeze. Then Odd turned his attention to Aspinall. He frowned when he saw the flask filled with light. A quick glance at Mirabelle told him all he needed to know, as did the fact that there were three guns pointing at him. With a lightness on his feet that was almost comical, Odd skipped backwards into the portal and it closed behind him, leaving Winthropp alone in the centre of the room.

Everyone in the room focused on him now. His silver eyes appraised the situation from within his hood.

One of the men raised his gun, but Winthropp simply held his palm out, and a bolt of silver flame shot through the air and threw the man right off his feet.

Shots rang out, and everyone scattered. 'Over here!' Mirabelle shouted, pulling Billy and Meg towards the back of the machine. Courtney was spun round in the confusion and fell to the ground. Billy ran straight for him, grabbed him and dragged him after Mirabelle and Meg. He pushed him into a sitting position up against the machine beside the two girls. Silver fire shot through the air, scorching the walls, while bullets whizzed past. One of them *spang*ed off the metal surface of the machine and missed Billy's head by inches.

Something plummeted from above and landed right at Mirabelle's feet.

The pied raven looked up at Mirabelle and cawed at her. Mirabelle was too taken aback to do or say anything.

'Look!' shouted Billy.

Another portal was opening just a few feet in front of them. Odd stepped through it. He bent forward, his hands on his thighs, gasping for air. He pointed at the portal.

'They won't listen to me, but they'll listen to you,' he said to Mirabelle.

Another bullet struck the machine, and they all jumped as one. A sudden line of silver flame flashed past and a man screamed.

'I asked for help!' Odd shouted, then covered his head as a bullet hit the wall behind him, sending a clump of white plaster spinning down.

Abelard rose up and started flying back and forth in front of the portal, cawing frantically.

Mirabelle recognised that kind of caw. She focused on the portal. She understood instinctively what needed to be done. After all, she could already sense them.

And so she called them.

The sound rumbled from the portal, dark and thunderous.

Then hundreds of ravens exploded out of it.

They swirled around the room, cawing ferociously, forming fierce lines of black that plunged down towards Aspinall and his henchmen.

Mirabelle leapt to her feet and looked round the side of the machine. She watched the ravens hurl themselves at the now frantic men. There were so many birds in the room that it was just a thick cloud of fizzing black.

A guard ran past, beating at one of his arms, which was burning with silver fire, headed for the open door. Mirabelle could see the other two already running out of the door, pursued by ravens, and Winthropp bent over, clutching his arm.

And, through a gap, she saw the white face of Aspinall, eyes bulging in terror as he flailed at the ravens with one hand, while protecting the flask of light with the other. He too stumbled towards the door. Mirabelle concentrated, and a clump of ravens broke away and headed straight for him, forcing him into a hasty retreat.

Meanwhile, Thorne was moving through the waves of ravens as if they weren't there, his eyes fixed on Aspinall. He was on him in seconds, and he grabbed him by the shoulder and spun him round. Aspinall snarled at him, and just for a split second his eyes went jet black and his face contorted into something feral and inhuman.

The sight made Mirabelle pull up in shock. It had the same effect on Thorne, who hesitated just long enough for Aspinall to kick him in the stomach. Thorne flew backwards across the ground, further than any kick from a human being had the right to send him.

Aspinall ran out through the door. Mirabelle chased after him.

Outside was grey and overcast, and Mirabelle found herself buffeted by a spiralling wind that was building in strength. Aspinall was halfway to the house, no doubt with his escape route already planned. Mirabelle tried to accelerate, but the man was moving with surprising speed. Just as she thought she would lose him altogether, a shout rang out:

'STOP!'

Mirabelle felt a scorching cold blaze through the grey fug. A line of silver fire sped across the courtyard and curved in front of Aspinall, blocking his route to the house. The flame arced round him in a horseshoe shape. Mirabelle turned to see Winthropp and Odd beside her. Winthropp was still clutching his arm, but he managed to raise his head and sniff the air.

'Just as I suspected,' he said.

Both Odd and Mirabelle exchanged a puzzled look.

'You've been hiding your true face,' Winthropp said to Aspinall.

Mirabelle looked at Aspinall. He had the tube gripped under one arm and he was snarling with fury. She saw his eyes blacken again, and she understood now what Winthropp had detected as Aspinall's features started to run and change.

'You're just like me and Billy,' she said. 'You're Misbegotten too.'

The creature called Aspinall now stood before them in all his glory. He had long curved talons that seemed to have yellowed and cracked with age. His face was grey and pocked. His teeth were sharp, but some of them were missing. His hair was long but thinning to a bright white fuzz. Mirabelle knew enough to recognise that he was very sick, possibly even dying.

'How old *are* you?' she asked, stepping towards him, ignoring the cold, searing lick of flame.

Aspinall snorted. To Mirabelle he now just looked pathetic and small.

'Old enough,' he replied, his voice a wretched croak.

'Are you dying?' asked Mirabelle.

Aspinall flinched at the question and hunched his shoulders. Mirabelle in her quiet fury was pleased to see him react this way. It felt as if she'd landed a physical blow. She was aware that someone was approaching. She turned to see Courtney standing a few feet behind her.

'You promised me,' he said to Aspinall. 'You promised.'

Aspinall snorted and turned his face away from him in disgust. Instead, he fixed his inky black eyes on Mirabelle. 'Dying? No. I refuse. I refuse!' he shouted, and Mirabelle could hear the fear in his voice.

'You used Mr Courtney to create your machine so you could save yourself.'

'The man's a fool. He has no idea of the potential this essence has.'

'We're Misbegotten – we die. You should accept that. I have.'

We. Even though she'd used the word she felt a certain disgust. The thought that she and this repellent creature might have something in common disturbed her.

Aspinall laughed. 'Poor child, poor foolish child. You know so little.'

'Tell me,' she said.

'Tell you what?' he said, eyeing her with suspicion.

'What's it been like?'

His face twitched and he tried to sneer, but Mirabelle could see something else in his eyes.

'You've been alone, haven't you?' she said.

Aspinall seemed to be struggling with something. 'Of course,' he hissed. 'Outcasts and freaks, that's all we are to them.'

We. Us. Aspinall seemed intent on using those words to try and convince Mirabelle that they were both kindred in some way. She found him contemptible and yet oddly pitiable, but as piteous as he appeared now she reminded herself of the cruelty he had inflicted. He would have to pay for his crimes. Her pity soured to anger again. She looked skyward where the ravens were now gathering anew. Aspinall saw her glance and reacted quickly, raising the flask over his head.

'NO!' Courtney screamed.

Aspinall hurled the flask and it shattered on the ground. A golden vapour swirled up from it. Aspinall put his head back and inhaled it.

Mirabelle could barely look. This vapour was all that remained of Piglet, and here was this creature ingesting it for his own ends. For just a moment her mind flashed back to something similar from years before. The eyes of the Malice. Its howling mouth.

Aspinall sucked in streams of the vapour through his mouth and nostrils. When it was all gone, he shivered for a moment, then lurched backwards as if he might fall. He steadied himself, opened his eyes and smiled. Mirabelle could already see the changes in his eyes. They gleamed, and his skin was losing its pock marks, becoming smoother. His teeth whitened, his talons became sharp and smooth.

Aspinall looked at his hands. 'Wonderful,' he said. 'Wonderful.'

Courtney was on his knees, sobbing.

'Get away from that thing!' someone shouted.

Mirabelle turned to see a grimacing Thorne limping from the building. He went down on one knee, clutching his chest, no doubt still winded from Aspinall's blow. He beckoned wildly to Mirabelle. 'Away!' was all he could manage.

She shook her head at him and turned her attention back to Aspinall.

Aspinall grinned. 'Restored to the height of my health. How marvellous.'

Mirabelle clenched a fist, conscious of the ravens wheeling overhead, but something stayed her hand for a moment. She needed to know more about this creature, despite her anger. She took a step towards Aspinall.

'You were afraid of dying, then. Was that it? Is that what all of this was about?' she asked, barely concealing her contempt.

Aspinall snarled, but there was no mistaking the look of shame on his face.

'It's understandable,' said Mirabelle. 'I've seen the fear that surrounds death. I know how frightening it must be for some people to come face to face with it, even for those who are immortal and have to stand by and watch their friends die.'

Aspinall nodded. 'You're very astute for one who looks so young.'

'I'm Misbegotten. I'm older than I look – and I'll age

too, maybe even die. But I'm not like you. I'm not afraid of it.'

Aspinall was busy now inspecting the tops of his hands. 'Oh my dear, there's so much you don't know about what it means to be what we are.'

'Stop saying *we*,' said Mirabelle.

'Why?' asked a smirking Aspinall.

Mirabelle didn't have a chance to answer. Aspinall suddenly spasmed and arched his back. '*Ugh*,' he grunted, 'that's . . . *ugh*.'

He jerked again, and it looked as if he were losing control of his limbs. He started to convulse, and Mirabelle heard something crack like bone.

Golden mist started to rise from him, as if seeping out of his skin, and as it emerged Aspinall began to wither. His body became twisted and gnarled. His hair became white again. This time his face was lined with even more wrinkles. He began to wheeze.

'What's happening to me?' he wailed.

The vapour rose in the air, becoming denser. It floated towards Mirabelle, condensing into something solid. Something with arms and legs, and a face. A face that Mirabelle recognised.

'Piglet!' Mirabelle cried.

Piglet stood before her. His boyish eyes and quiet almost contemplative demeanour was restored. Mirabelle grabbed him, squeezed him tight and felt the warmth of tears on her face. Piglet wrapped his arms loosely around her, as if unsure of what exactly he was supposed to do in response.

Over his shoulder, she could see Aspinall totter towards them, his clawed hand outstretched.

He shrieked. 'You can't! I won't let you take what's mine. I won't!'

Mirabelle looked at Courtney on his knees, shuddering and weeping. She saw a struggling Thorne pushing himself up to try to break into a run. Winthropp was still on the ground, clutching his injured arm and hissing in pain.

Aspinall was almost upon them, his claws outstretched. Mirabelle could see the fear and panic in his eyes.

Something black swirled into existence behind Aspinall.

Mirabelle hugged Piglet to her, tensing for a blow. She felt a rush of air as Billy leapt from behind her.

He collided with Aspinall, sending him hurtling into the portal that had formed behind him. Aspinall screamed. The portal snapped shut.

Billy dropped down on to his haunches, panting, Odd bending over him in concern.

Mirabelle looked at Odd.

'Where did you send him?'

Aspinall beat his fists against the thick glass of the Vulsifier. His voice was faint, but there was no mistaking the rage on his face.

'What do we do with him?' Odd asked.

'Leave him in there,' snarled Thorne.

'For how long?'

'Until he rots.'

Mirabelle's expression hardened. 'Then we're as bad as he is. He has to pay for what he did, but not like this.'

Thorne looked unsure of himself. In the rafters above, a silent congregation of ravens watched impassively, while Piglet observed the exchange with a faint look of curiosity.

'He's dangerous,' said Winthropp.

'I agree,' said Billy.

Mirabelle stepped towards the viewing window and looked at Aspinall. 'He's afraid,' she said.

Courtney was back in his chair, looking inconsolable. He gave a feeble wave of his cane. 'Do what you must with him. He betrayed me.'

'You're not the only one who knows about betrayal,' said Mirabelle. She looked at Billy, who was holding Meg's hand. 'It's hard, but you can forgive it.'

Billy gave a slight nod in gratitude.

'I don't know,' said Odd. 'It's not as if we have somewhere we can put him.'

'What's he saying?' asked Winthropp, leaning closer to the glass.

'He's threatening us,' said Billy, holding Meg closer. 'He says he's going to put us all in the machine, starting with Mirabelle.'

Thorne leapt forward and pulled down the lever. Mirabelle launched herself at him and grabbed his arm, but it was too late. The colours started to snap and spark like lightning within the chamber. The machine hummed and trembled. Thorne looked fiercely at Aspinall as he hurled himself against the glass in an effort to escape. Thorne's hand was still pressing down on the lever, and nothing Mirabelle did could remove it.

'Stop it! Stop it!' she shouted, pulling at his fingers and beating his hand.

But it was too late. Aspinall was already turning to dust. He looked in horror at his own hands as his fingers disintegrated. He raised his head, his dark eyes fixed on Mirabelle, and the lower half of his face fell away like a clump of sand rolling down a dune. His eyes implored her for mercy, and they were filled with terror.

Soon there was nothing but dust wafting through the chamber. Thorne rammed the lever upwards, and the machine juddered and fell silent.

Piglet

Piglet considers all that has happened. He remembers stepping into the machine, the sense of separation, the fear, yet also knowing instinctively that this was the only way forward, the only way to make things right. There was no pain, just a sense of letting go. And for a while there was only darkness.

And Piglet drifted in a soothing silence.

Then gradually, piece by piece, the world came back.

And all the moments before, especially the moment he stepped into the machine, have led him here.

He watches now as Mirabelle hits Thorne again and again. The look on his face is one of sorrow and guilt. He stands helpless against the onslaught, unwilling to defend himself. Piglet doesn't understand why, but he understands Mirabelle a little better. He knows she feels sorry for the creature that was Aspinall, despite her anger over what he did. This makes sense to Piglet, especially after occupying Aspinall's mind. The creature may have been cruel, but he was also pitiable, lost, alone.

Piglet has known these feelings himself.

Now he does what he must. Besides, he is curious.

He inhales.

Exhales.

Dissipates.

He enters Courtney's mind first. After all he is the key. He sees snatches of a life. Images of a once strong and proud man brought low by loss. Houses, cars, crystal chandeliers. Courtney smiling.

Then a black night punctured by blazes of light, the air trembling. The howl of air raid sirens.

Courtney's face twisted in grief and pain.

A coffin lowered into a grave. Sunlight glinting off its polished mahogany, like a mockery. And Courtney standing by the grave. He has only one thing left . . .

Thorne is next. Another lost soul filled with self-loathing. Piglet sees him trudging through a barren landscape. His world is grey and haunted. And then suddenly there is light in his world, warmth and hope, a dazzling smile and . . .

Alice . . .

And Thorne's world flares to a brilliant brightness and he soars now and knows happiness.

Real happiness.

But the darkness returns. Piglet sees Thorne in a cellar, looking at the tools of his trade. The rune-covered weapons and traps. He is a hunter of monsters. His own kind fear him. And because of that he believes he is the worst monster of all, and he is unworthy of happiness, even with the promise of a child. What good can he bring to the life of a child, he wonders. He is angry, and he hates himself, and he is afraid he will not be enough.

So he runs.

And Odd is afraid. And Mirabelle is afraid. And Piglet already knows Billy's fear.

Fear. It is a thing they all share. Fear of losing someone precious. It makes them hide, makes them betray, makes them lash out, makes them hurt themselves. And, in the case of one person in particular, it makes them devote every ounce of their being to one thing.

Piglet leaves them. He returns to himself.

A shocked-looking Thorne is trying to support his weight against the side of the machine. Mirabelle looks at him with a newfound understanding. Odd looks dazed.

And all eyes turn to Courtney. He looks as if he wants to run and hide. But there is no hiding now.

Piglet waits for them all by the door. It's time to show them. It's time to go to the room.

Mirabelle

Mirabelle watched the shallow rise and fall of the boy's chest as he lay asleep in the bed. Odd, Billy, Winthropp, Meg and Thorne stood silently by the door with her.

The bed seemed too large for him, and the room was lit by the glow of a single lamp, but it was clear to her how pale the boy's skin was, how sharp and pointed his cheekbones were.

Courtney stood over him, stroking his forehead with a trembling hand.

'Matthew is all I have left after his mother died during the Blitz. He's only twelve. He's all I . . .' He choked back a sob.

Mirabelle nodded.

'There's no cure for what he has?' she said.

Courtney shook his head.

'And you thought Piglet's essence might save his life,' said Mirabelle.

Courtney looked at them all defiantly. 'Hate me if you want, but I did what I had to for the sake of my son.'

'I don't hate you,' said Mirabelle.

Courtney was fighting back tears. 'Everything I did was for nothing.'

Piglet stepped towards the bed. Odd frowned at Mirabelle. Courtney looked surprised.

'What are you doing?' he asked.

Piglet held the boy's hand and closed his eyes. He frowned as he concentrated, then swayed, looking for an awful moment as if he might fall forward. Mirabelle had to fight the urge to go to him.

'What's he doing?' Courtney called plaintively.

No one spoke. They were too busy focusing on Piglet. Mirabelle wondered if the others saw what she saw. A soft golden light underneath Piglet's skin travelled into Matthew's hand and up his arm. It shimmered for a moment, then faded . . .

Piglet let go, opened his eyes and sighed.

Mirabelle noticed that Matthew wasn't as pale any more. His eyes opened, took a few moments to focus, then he smiled as he saw his father.

Courtney rushed to his side and grabbed his hand, then

he hugged him fiercely, sobbing with joy.

'I think it's time for us to leave,' said Mirabelle.

Odd opened a portal in the courtyard. The wind had died down. Mirabelle stood a few feet away from the others, looking up at Thorne. The anger and disgust she'd felt towards him at first had all but ebbed away, and thanks to Piglet it felt as if she were seeing him a little more clearly. He was a wounded man, burdened by self-hatred, but she knew now that there was good in him, despite everything. Abelard was perched on his shoulder, his head jerking from side to side as if he were pretending not to listen in on their conversation.

'You can come with us.'

Thorne shook his head. 'Wouldn't be right,' he muttered. 'Not after the things I've done.'

'You'd be welcome to stay. You know you would. I can explain to the others – or I can get Piglet to explain. Once they understand everything about you, they'll be happy for you to be part of the Family – I'm sure they will.'

Thorne gave a half-hearted scowl.

'I know,' she said. 'Thanks to Piglet I know everything. You're not an outcast, and you would have been . . .' She paused. 'You could be a good father.'

Thorne struggled to look at her. 'Not yet,' he said hoarsely.

Mirabelle nodded. 'You're not ready. I understand. Piglet showed me that too. Just so you know, we never turn anyone away from Rookhaven. Not ever. *She* knew that – that's why she came.'

Thorne started to move off.

'I met her, you know.'

Thorne froze. He looked at Mirabelle, blinking in astonishment. 'How?'

'Doesn't matter. But I did meet her, and . . . and she was . . .' Mirabelle swallowed back tears.

'Beautiful,' said Thorne, and for the first time the darkness lifted from his eyes, and he gave a faint smile.

'He's not coming?' said Billy as Mirabelle approached them. He watched Thorne slouch away, Abelard flapping on his shoulder.

'No,' said Mirabelle. 'Not just yet.'

'A pity, I'm sure he'd be wonderfully witty company,' said Odd.

Mirabelle gave him a withering look, and Odd looked suitably chastened.

She turned to Winthropp, who was still clutching his arm. 'How bad is it?'

Winthropp shook his head. 'It's just a graze. It will heal in less than a day.'

'Thank you, Winthropp. Thank you for all your help.'

Winthropp gave a gracious nod.

'Are you ready?' Mirabelle asked Billy.

Billy took half a step back, one hand on Meg's shoulder. 'Ready for what?'

'To go home.'

Billy

Billy experienced a certain trepidation as they all stepped through the portal. The hairs on the back of his neck stood on end, and there was a sensation of being pulled forward. He gripped Meg's hand tightly, and tried to give her a reassuring look, but she was smiling happily.

When he looked up, they were already in the hall of the House of Rookhaven. He felt a moment of dizziness, and then a voice by his ear said:

'You're back.'

Gideon appeared out of thin air and grinned at him with a mouth filled with pointed teeth.

'I see you caused quite a bit of trouble. But I'm guessing you must have been forgiven, otherwise Mirabelle wouldn't be with you. Although she does have very low standards. She can put up with anyone, I suppose, even me.'

He went down on one knee in front of Meg.

'And who's this?'

'This is Meg, my sister,' Billy replied, still reeling a little from their sudden arrival, and at Gideon's surprisingly affable manner.

Gideon shook Meg's hand. 'How do you do, Meg? You're very welcome. This is the House of Rookhaven. I'm known as a bit of a troublemaker, but the world needs troublemakers. That's what I think, anyway. Don't listen to what anyone else tells you.'

With that, he vanished. Meg clapped her hands together with delight.

Billy tensed when he saw Enoch emerge from the shadows. Eliza was with him.

'Look at him glowering,' Odd whispered. 'He's always glowering.'

'We did it, Uncle. We rescued Piglet,' said Mirabelle.

Enoch looked pleased for a second, then frowned as he looked at Mirabelle. 'You left without permission. You put yourself and others in danger.'

'She made a snap decision. It turned out to be the correct one. I think she is to be commended,' said Winthropp.

There was a moment when almost everybody present looked at Winthropp in surprise.

'How generous of you, Winthropp,' said Eliza.

Winthropp nodded graciously.

Enoch pointed at Billy. 'Correct or not, the boy must be punished for his transgression.'

Billy was surprised when Mirabelle took his hand in hers.

'No, Uncle, we've brought him home. This is where Billy and his sister, Meg, belong now.'

Enoch looked perplexed, but Eliza seemed pleased. More people started to emerge from the shadows. Billy fought the urge to run as he caught sight of the Dibbles and spotted Daisy and Dotty materialising from a wall.

Meg peered round his leg at them, her eyes wide.

Billy heard the high reedy tones of Uncle Urg ask, 'What's going on, Siegfried?'

'He took Piglet from us, and you think he can just walk back in here without consequences?' said Enoch.

'Yes, Uncle, I do,' replied Mirabelle. 'He's earned it.'

He gave her a dour look. 'I remain unconvinced. I would like an explanation for your rather dubious reasoning.'

'Well then, you shall have one, Uncle,' said Mirabelle. 'Piglet!' she called.

Piglet stepped forward. He raised his hands, closed his eyes and his form dissipated, becoming a revolving column of golden light. There were a couple of shrieks of protest at first, but then Billy noticed how entranced the audience became as the golden light shone on their faces.

'Piglet will explain,' said Mirabelle.

And with that Piglet moved forward like a wave and embraced Enoch, Eliza and the rest of the onlookers. Within moments they all understood everything.

Mirabelle turned to Billy, and he felt as if his heart might burst when she smiled and said: 'Welcome home, Billy Catchpole.'

Mirabelle

Mirabelle would never forget the last occasion she'd walked to Dr Ellenby's, but it was different this time. She'd been surprised when Odd had offered to accompany her, especially now, during daylight. He was remarkably chatty, even for him, which of course was a sign that he was nervous about something. She listened patiently to him, nodding in all the right places, and she noticed how he kept one hand in his right pocket at all times. Even Lucius was well behaved as he perched quietly on her shoulder.

'What's that you've got?' she asked.

'Nothing,' he said. 'Nothing important.' And he went right back to fidgeting with whatever the 'nothing' was in his pocket.

She shared his hesitation when they reached the door. They glanced at each other in understanding, both knowing what the other was feeling, and how this moment reminded them of that terrible day. How it was like a bridge that must be crossed. Odd stepped forward and rapped the knocker.

Dr Davenport looked delighted to see them when he opened the door. He ushered them both into the study. Mirabelle caught the nervous looks he gave her, and she supposed she didn't blame him, considering her previous treatment of him.

He and Odd were laughing about something Dr Ellenby had once said when she stepped towards him.

'Paul?' she said.

He looked genuinely taken aback by her use of his first name. He looked even more surprised when she held the pipe out in her hand.

'This is yours,' she said.

Dr Davenport shook his head. 'No, no, he would have wanted you to have it . . .'

'Take it, please,' said Mirabelle. 'It belongs here, with you.'

He took it from her and smiled gratefully. She was secretly delighted later on when he lit it without even thinking as they continued to talk and laugh.

Mirabelle was surprised by how light her spirits felt when she, Odd and Lucius left the house. They had an unspoken understanding about walking home rather than using a portal. Mirabelle preferred it. Walking seemed so much more respectful and natural when visiting. They were halfway home when Odd stopped talking, a sure sign that he was preoccupied with something.

Mirabelle sighed. 'Just go.'

'What?'

'I know that look. Just go.'

'I don't know what you mean.' He looked guilty for a moment. 'Well, I do have an errand to run. It's something I've been putting off for quite a while.'

A portal formed behind him, but he seemed reluctant to move.

'Odd?'

'You know when you have to do something important, and it's sort of difficult, but you know you'll do it, because you promised yourself?'

Mirabelle took him by the shoulders and turned him round to face the portal.

'Go,' she said.

Odd took a deep breath, then stepped into the portal. It winked out of existence.

Mirabelle felt a gust of wind behind her, and the day darkened slightly. Lucius started flapping and cawing as if in protest.

'To what do I owe the pleasure, Uncle?' said Mirabelle, turning to greet Enoch.

He stepped towards her, reached inside his jacket and took out an envelope, which he handed to her.

Mirabelle recognised Jem's handwriting immediately, and her heart leapt.

'It just arrived. I decided it was best that you read it as soon as possible. You've been waiting long enough.'

'Thank you, Uncle,' she said. It took all her willpower not to open it there and then.

Enoch nodded and cleared his throat. 'They're settling in.'

'Billy and Meg? Yes.'

Enoch focused on some imaginary fluff on his collar. 'I was angry at first with the boy, but I understand now why he did what he did.'

'Thanks to Piglet,' said Mirabelle, smiling at Enoch's discomfort. She knew he wasn't the best at expressing his feelings.

'Yes, Piglet revealed quite a bit to everyone,' he said, slightly ruefully. He gazed into the middle distance, and neither of them spoke for a moment.

'I saw your father,' said Enoch, without looking at her.

'Oh?' said Mirabelle, trying to keep her voice even.

'Yes, once again I have Piglet to thank for that.' Enoch frowned. 'He seemed lost, somewhat alone. I think he feels guilty. Guilty perhaps about not doing everything he could to protect you. I think in that regard he and I have quite a bit in common.'

'Your guilt is misplaced, Uncle. I think you're being a little too hard on yourself, just like my father,' said Mirabelle, smiling at him.

'He would be welcome if he came to Rookhaven, just as Billy and Meg are. Just as welcome as Jem and Tom were.'

'Thank you, Uncle. That's very generous of you.'

Enoch placed a hand over his pendant and bowed slightly. He spread his wings and took flight. Mirabelle watched him ascend, shielding her eyes from the sun with her hand.

'I think it's time we were getting back, Lucius.'

Lucius cawed and Mirabelle looked at the envelope. She made a solemn promise to herself not to read the contents until she got home.

It didn't take her long to break that promise.

Odd

Odd paced back and forth on the hill overlooking the fishing village. Moonlight played on the water as it always did. He could almost name each ripple, he had seen them so many times. The same *clink clink* sounds wafted on the warm breeze. The same owl hooted at the same time it always did.

'Right, all right,' he muttered to himself, trying to muster his courage. His fingers closed round the object in his pocket. That seemed to decide the matter for him. He straightened up, inhaled the night air and watched the moon disappear behind a cloud. He focused on his destination, a street not too far from this very hill, then he opened up a portal.

The portal took him to the roof of a house in the centre of the fishing village. He sat on the edge, dangling his legs as if swinging off a pier. He felt nervous, and he thought back on how he'd almost confessed everything about his 'refuge' to Winthropp on his previous visit.

The village was quiet. There was no one about. The pubs had closed. Everyone was in bed.

Well, almost everyone.

He heard steps coming down the cobbled street and saw a young man turn round the corner.

The man stopped directly under him, just as he always

did when Odd came here at this exact moment, in this exact place. The man fumbled around inside his jacket, mumbling something to himself. Everything was exactly the same. Nothing had changed. And nothing ever would.

Until now.

Odd cleared his throat.

'Hello,' said Odd.

The man looked more mildly surprised than startled.

'Hello,' he replied. 'What a strange place to be.'

'Yes,' said Odd, 'but surprisingly comfy on a night like tonight.'

The young man squinted up at him, but Odd knew he was obscured by shadow, and would remain so as the moon stayed behind the clouds. Which it would for a full five minutes. He'd already counted on several earlier visits.

The man nodded as if to concede the fact. 'Perhaps. It is rather a lovely night.'

'You like to wander, then?'

'Indeed I do,' said the man, rummaging again inside his jacket.

'I'm quite partial to a bit of a wander myself,' said Odd.

The man had taken a pipe out of his jacket. He pointed it at Odd. 'Are roofs your favoured destination?'

'Tonight this one is.'

There was a surprisingly warm and genial pause. The man waved his pipe around.

'Helps me think,' he said.

'Wandering?'

'Yes.'

'Me too. What were you thinking about?'

The man frowned. 'Life, I suppose. Endings.'

Odd swallowed. 'I see. What prompted that if you don't mind me asking?'

The man pursed his lips and frowned, as if considering how best to proceed.

'I lost someone,' he said. 'She died. I . . . well, there was nothing to be done. Nothing I or anyone else could do.'

He scratched his forehead.

'I'm sorry,' said Odd.

The man waved his apology away.

'No, really, I am,' said Odd. 'An old friend of mine used to say to me that it's the temporariness of things that makes them precious. If that's any consolation. Maybe it isn't.'

'Your friend sounds very wise.'

'He is, was, I mean.'

The man frowned. 'Do I know you?'

Yes, Odd wanted to say. *Yes you know me. You're one of my oldest, dearest friends and I miss you, and I'm sorry.*

Odd suddenly found it hard to speak. He shrugged and squinted into the dark.

'Would you like to come down?'

'I'm fine up here, thank you.'

'Are you sure you won't join me?'

'Maybe another time.'

The man looked confused by the comment.

Odd exhaled. 'Were you thinking about anything else?'

'As a matter of fact I was. I was thinking about a career.'

'You should try medicine. I think you'd be good at it.'

The man looked slightly gobsmacked. 'What an extraordinary thing to say. I was just thinking about that.'

Odd waved a hand in his direction. 'It's just that you look like a medical person, and you . . . you have a pleasant manner.'

Odd winced at his words.

The man mused on what he'd said and seemed to take it as a compliment.

Odd reached into his pocket. 'I have something for you. A gift.'

He threw the packet of tobacco, and the man snatched it deftly from the air. He examined it, then waved in thanks.

'Very kind of you.'

'I know you've run out.'

The man opened the packet of tobacco and filled his pipe with it. Odd watched him as he lit his pipe, the glow from the bowl lighting up his features and reflecting off his spectacles. He threw his match into the night and it glowed a fierce orange for a moment before vanishing.

'I should be on my way,' he said. He tapped a finger to his forehead in salutation. 'It was very nice talking to you. Thank you so much for the gift.'

'My pleasure,' said Odd.

Odd stood up and watched as the man walked on into the night.

'Goodbye, Marcus,' he whispered.

Piglet

Deep, deep down, in the darkness of his room, Piglet is thinking.

He thinks about what he's seen and what he's felt. The images and feelings of those around him, of those he calls family.

Family. Such a small word, and yet so huge also. Piglet thinks he is beginning to understand words now. Their significance. Their power.

He thinks about fear. Odd's fear of losing a friend. Billy's fear of losing his sister. He feels it all, knows it all. It is part of him now, and knowing it makes him feel strangely content. Because, even though there is fear, there is something to counteract it, something just as powerful.

Family.

He misses Dr Ellenby, but even that is tinged with a strange happiness because Dr Ellenby was his friend, and Piglet feels privileged to have been in the world with him, to have shared his thoughts and dreams.

And now Piglet looks beyond his room.

Outside, a scrap of darkness wheels through the night sky. It searches for its destination. Finds it. Fixes on it.

Mirabelle is in her room, smiling as she writes a letter. She looks up and puts down her pen, frowning as if sensing something. Piglet sees her leave her room, sees her walking the corridors of the house. Wandering, as if searching for something she has lost.

The house is unnaturally quiet. It is as if it knows she must be alone in this moment.

Piglet smiles. He knows what comes next.

Mirabelle stands in a shaft of moonlight, and just for a moment the light flickers as something passes over the face of the moon.

Mirabelle looks up into the night sky and her heart skips a beat.

Piglet is glad because he can sense that Mirabelle already knows. Somehow deep down she has always known.

The pied raven is coming.

The End

Acknowledgements

A big thank you to everyone at Macmillan Children's Books for making this book a reality. Thank you Venetia, Sam, and Krystle, and thank you Jo, Clare and everyone on the communications and marketing team who helped introduce the monsters to the world.

Edward Bettison has outdone himself with the illustrations. Thanks again Ed for your breathtaking work. Thank you also Rachel Vale for your beautiful design work.

A special thank you to the librarians, booksellers, readers and teachers on Twitter who responded so kindly and generously to the world and characters I created.

My eternal thanks to Sophie Hicks, agent, friend, legend.